**Praise for the**

## Maggie Brooklyn Mysteries

# Secrets at the Chocolate Mansion

"Maggie is smart and witty, with an inquisitive mind. . . . There are a lot of surprises and twists throughout the story. A solid choice for mystery fans." —*School Library Journal*

# Vanishing Acts

"Witty and resourceful, compassionate and lovable, Maggie is just the kind of girl you want . . . to relate to. And she lives right next door." —*Park Slope Reader*

"Perfect for fans . . . of Judy Moody or Allie Finkle and mystery fans who enjoy Sammy Keyes." —*School Library Journal*

# Girl's Best Friend

"This is my kind of book! . . . It's surprise after surprise, with lots of twists and turns." —R. L. Stine, author of Goosebumps

"A barking good mystery." —*Discovery Girls*

"Leslie Margolis has found the perfect mix—a city story, a tween story, *and* a mystery that truly keeps you guessing." —Gordon Korman, author of *The 39 Clues: The Emperor's Code* and *Framed*

## Books by Leslie Margolis

THE MAGGIE BROOKLYN MYSTERIES

*Girl's Best Friend*

*Vanishing Acts*

*Secrets at the Chocolate Mansion*

◆ ◆ ◆

THE ANNABELLE UNLEASHED SERIES

*Boys Are Dogs*

*Girls Acting Catty*

*Everybody Bugs Out*

*One Tough Chick*

*Monkey Business*

a maggie brooklyn mystery

# Secrets at the Chocolate Mansion

Leslie Margolis



BLOOMSBURY
NEW YORK LONDON OXFORD NEW DELHI SYDNEY

First published in the United States of America in September 2013
by Bloomsbury Children's Books
Paperback edition published in September 2014
www.bloomsbury.com

Bloomsbury is a registered trademark of Bloomsbury Publishing Plc

For information about permission to reproduce selections from this book, write to Permissions, Bloomsbury Children's Books, 1385 Broadway, New York, New York 10018
Bloomsbury books may be purchased for business or promotional use. For information on bulk purchases please contact Macmillan Corporate and Premium Sales Department at specialmarkets@macmillan.com

Library of Congress Cataloging-in-Publication Data
Margolis, Leslie.
Secrets at the chocolate mansion : a Maggie Brooklyn mystery / Leslie Margolis.
pages cm
Summary: Maggie Brooklyn is distracted from solving the mystery of who is out to sabotage the new sweet shop in the neighborhood because her new babysitting job has her and her twin brother, Finn, spending time in what may be a real haunted mansion.
ISBN 978-1-61963-036-9 (hardcover) • ISBN 978-1-61963-177-9 (e-book)
[1. Brothers and sisters—Fiction. 2. Twins—Fiction. 3. Junior high schools—Fiction. 4. Schools—Fiction. 5. Dogs—Fiction. 6. Haunted houses—Fiction. 7. Ghosts—Fiction. 8. Mystery and detective stories.] I. Title.
PZ7.M33568Sec 2013 [Fic]—dc23 2013009608

---

ISBN 978-1-61963-493-0 (paperback)

Book design by Nicole Gastonguay
Typeset by Westchester Book Composition
Printed and bound in the U.S.A. by Berryville Graphics, Inc., Berryville, Virginia
4 6 8 10 9 7 5

All papers used by Bloomsbury Publishing, Inc., are natural, recyclable products made from wood grown in well-managed forests. The manufacturing processes conform to the environmental regulations of the country of origin.

*For Leo and Lucy and Jim*

*The lady doth protest too much, methinks.*

—Shakespeare, *Hamlet*

# Chapter 1

◆ ◆ ◆

I've never been good at double Dutch and I don't really care for Dubble Bubble gum. The sweetness only lasts for thirty seconds; after that, it tastes like it belongs on the underside of someone's desk. When people call my twin brother and me "double trouble," we both roll our eyes. Yet, somehow the prospect of a double date—a real, official double date—seemed different, thrilling, and full of new possibility. I mean, who knew what would happen? I'll tell you who: no one.

That's why I felt so bouncy on Saturday afternoon, just about ready to bubble over with enthusiasm. Enthusiasm I worked hard to hide, because come on, it's okay to be super excited about a date with your boyfriend, but it's not exactly cool to show it. Especially when you're in seventh grade.

Acting cool and calm was harder than usual on

account of the fact that our friend Sonya's mom had just opened up an old-fashioned soda fountain and we were on our way to the grand opening. "We" meaning me and my boyfriend, Milo; my best friend, Lulu; and my brother, Finn.

Yep—that's right. My best friend and my twin brother are a couple. It's a long story.

I think.

Actually, I don't know whether it's a long story or not. They've kept me in the dark about most of their relationship, and I'm happy about that.

I'm still getting used to the fact that they're together; I don't want to know details. Not that any of that bothered me today. My homework was done, my weekend chores were complete, and there was nowhere else I wanted to be on this brilliantly sunny Saturday afternoon. It was the perfect day for an ice cream soda, or a root beer float, or a famous Brooklyn Egg Cream, all of which would be available at Sonya's Sweets in just a few short moments. Or at least that's what we'd been told.

"Sonya's so lucky. Having a candy store named after you has got to be the best thing in the world," Lulu said as we strolled down Seventh Avenue toward President Street.

"If I ever open up a candy store, I'll totally name it

after you," Finn told her. He ran his hand through his long, dark, shaggy hair.

Finn pays way more attention to his hair when Lulu is around, I've noticed. He also spends tons of time getting ready in the morning, even though his wardrobe hasn't changed. He still wears the same basic outfits: jeans or cords and T-shirts; his thin, gray hoodie when it gets cold outside; and a navy-blue puffy vest for the coldest days of winter. It simply takes him much longer to put them on these days.

Lulu grabbed his hand and bumped shoulders with him, gazing at him with the goofiest expression I've ever seen.

I worked hard to keep from rolling my eyes, but allowed myself a small smirk. Milo caught my expression and raised his eyebrows.

"Saw that, Maggie," he whispered.

I could tell he thought I was being too critical of them, but I wasn't about to admit it. "Saw what?" I asked with a shrug.

Milo just shook his head and laughed.

"Lulu's is the perfect name for a candy store," said Finn. "It's short and to the point."

Lulu crinkled her nose. "Don't you mean short, to the point, and way too boring?"

"Sorry," said Finn. "Have you got a better idea?"

"Sure," said Lulu, thinking for a moment. "Lucky Lulu's."

"What's lucky about it?" asked Milo.

"The fact that I have a candy store," Lulu said, as though it were obvious.

"How about Lulu's Lollipops?" I asked. "There's alliteration there, at least."

"Alliter-what?" asked Finn.

"Alliteration," I repeated. "You know—when two words start with the same sound. That thing we've been studying in English all week."

"Come on, Maggie. It's Saturday," said Finn. "Let's not talk about school."

"Using a word I recently learned in school hardly constitutes 'talking about school,'" I pointed out. "Right, Milo?"

Milo grinned at me and shook his head slowly. "I'm not getting in between you and Finn."

"Lulu?" I asked.

My friend laughed in my face. (Nice, huh?) "You're asking me to take sides between my best friend and my boyfriend? No way."

"How is it a fight when there's only one answer?" I asked.

"Let's talk about candy stores some more," said Lulu. "Lulu's Lollipops does sound cute, but won't it be misleading if I'm selling all types of candy?"

She had a good point, and I told her so. "Then how about Lulu's Lollipops and More?"

Lulu considered this as she twirled a strand of wavy black hair around her finger. "The 'More' is too vague. I could be selling tires or something."

"Tires and lollipops. Now there's an exciting concept for a business," Milo teased.

"Oh, sarcasm," Lulu said, her voice drenched in it. "I *love* sarcasm. Can't get enough of it. So please don't stop. Seriously. Keep it coming."

"Sorry," said Milo.

"No, I'm *totally* serious," she said, getting right up in his face. "Keep it up."

"Okay, I get it," Milo yelled, throwing up his hands. "Tough crowd."

"Oh, she's vicious," said Finn. "Be careful."

When Lulu socked Finn's shoulder, he said, "Yeeouch! See what I mean?"

"Hey, check it out," I said as we got closer. "That new sign looks amazing. You can see it from a block away."

"I think that's the point," said Finn.

"I know that," I said, shoving my brother. "I'm just saying, they did an awesome job."

"Sonya's dad made it," Lulu told us. "And I think it's more of a picture window than a sign. You know, since it makes up almost the entire glass storefront. He's really into stained glass. It took him months to finish because some of the materials had to be imported from Italy."

"That sounds serious," said Milo.

"Yeah. He just left yesterday to go to India for a whole month. He felt so bad about missing the opening that he went all out with the window," Lulu explained.

The sign—excuse me—the picture window was huge, with sparkly blue glass lettering. It also featured fluffy cupcakes, frosty milk shakes, and juicy pies. All of the food had arms and legs and looked as if it were in the middle of a dessert-inspired dance party.

"This is too excellent," said Lulu as she opened the door. She started to say something else but stopped as soon as she took in the scene.

I was speechless, too. Once inside, I felt like I'd stepped back in time, to the days when girls wore poodle skirts and boys greased back their hair and everybody listened to rock-and-roll music on the jukebox.

"This is incredible!" said Lulu. "Sonya's mom totally outdid herself."

She was right. Little round tables with elaborately curled iron chairs dotted the black-and-white checkered floor. Old-timey carved wooden signs hung on the walls. They read *ICE CREAM SODA 3 CENTS* and *SUNDAES FOR A NICKEL.*

"Think those are the real prices?" asked Finn.

"I wish," said Lulu.

"Wow, that's an awesome display," I said, pointing to the rack of penny candy opposite the cash register. It was filled with things like candy buttons, Turkish Taffy, Chick-O-Sticks, Wack-O-Wax lips, Ice Cubes chocolates, and a bunch of other stuff I hadn't ever seen before.

"I feel like I just walked into 1950," said Milo. "I half expect people to use words like 'golly-gee willickers' and 'okey-dokey.' "

"Do you think people actually said those things?" I wondered. "Because I've only heard them in movies."

"Good point," said Milo. "Maybe that's just how old-time teen-speak is depicted in movies and on TV."

"Speaking of," I said, "did you know that when we were little, Finn thought the entire world once existed in black and white, not color? It's all people saw before the invention of color television. Like television engineers invented not only color transmission, but the actual color spectrum."

Milo laughed. "For real?"

Lulu said, "That's adorable."

Finn grinned a sly grin. "It's true. And I have plenty of embarrassing Maggie stories I could tell," he warned. "Like, you all know how she feels about mice, right? Well, this one time when we rented a cabin in Maine . . ."

I decided this was the perfect moment to change the subject. "Oh, there's Sonya," I said, pointing to the back of the store.

Sonya stood behind the long white marble counter filling up straw holders with red-and-white-striped straws that looked like peppermint sticks. Her long dark hair was in two braids that hung over her shoulders. She wore a pink apron and a white paper hat, just like the other employees in the store.

As soon as she saw us, she beamed and waved at us to come closer.

Lulu and I reached over the counter for hugs, while the boys simply waved.

"Thanks for coming," Sonya said.

"Are you kidding? We wouldn't miss this," I told her. "How's it going? You look so grown-up. Love your hair, too."

"Oh, the braids are a requirement," said Sonya, tugging on one braid. "And speaking of official stuff—if the Department of Labor comes by and asks any questions, I do not actually work here because that would be illegal. I'm too young. I'm only helping my parents out on a volunteer basis."

"Okay, you may not be officially working," said Milo. "But you sure look like an authentic soda jerk."

"Who are you calling a jerk?" asked Sonya, hands on her hips, clearly offended.

Milo laughed. "I'm talking about your hat. That's what it's called—a soda-jerk hat."

"Oh, yeah. I knew that," said Sonya. Although clearly she didn't, because moments later she tilted her head to one side and asked, "If I'm wearing it, does that make me a jerk?"

"You couldn't be a jerk if you tried," I told Sonya. "You're as sweet as everything in that awesome candy display."

It's true, too. Sonya is all bright smiles and shiny rainbows. She's one of the nicest kids at Fiske Street Junior High, which is why she's one of my closest friends.

"Do you sell chocolate malteds?" asked Lulu, leaning her elbows on the counter.

"Of course we do," said Sonya. "Do you want one?"

"No," said Lulu. "I was just wondering if you had them."

"Didn't you see the picture of the chocolate malted in the window?" asked Sonya.

"The dancing one?" asked Lulu. "Of course. Except I figured maybe he was just for show. Or she. Which is it?"

"All of our malteds are gender-neutral. The shakes are a different story," Sonya told us, laughing at her own joke. "But what you guys should really do is try the pie. My mom is famous for them. There's a fresh one in the oven right now; should be ready in a few minutes."

Pie sounded pretty good. "What kind is it?" I asked.

"Strawberry rhubarb. My mom made ten of them from scratch this morning," Sonya said as she untied her apron strings and stepped out from behind the counter. "Follow me. I reserved the best booth for you guys. It's all the way in the back."

"Taking a break already?" Sonya's mom, Ricki, called from the other side of the store.

"I've been working since seven o'clock this morning," Sonya cried.

When Ricki laughed, I noticed she had the same smile as Sonya. Or vice versa, I suppose. "I'm kidding, sweetie. We've got things covered." She gestured toward the two other employees at the shop. One of them looked a lot like Sonya and her mom—same dark skin and big brown eyes. She wore her hair in braids, like Sonya. They could've been twins, except this girl was much taller. Older, too, I think. The other person was a white guy—tall, with long blond hair that hung down his back in a low ponytail.

"Who are they?" I asked.

Sonya pointed to the girl with braids. "That's my cousin Felicity. And the other guy is Joshua Marcus, who lives across the street."

"Oh, cool," I said with a nod. "I thought he looked familiar."

"He's cute, huh?" Sonya whispered to me.

"I guess." I shrugged. "It's hard for me to tell. I don't like old guys, so he's not really my type."

"He's only nineteen," said Sonya. "And I'll be thirteen in less than a month. And while a six-year age difference seems like a big deal now, when we're older, it's *so* not going to be. My mom is ten whole years younger than my dad."

"I don't know," I said, staring at Joshua. "Nineteen sounds ancient to me."

We made our way through the crowd to the back booth, which was empty except for the RESERVED sign on the table. Sonya plucked it up and slipped it into her back pocket.

"Wow, VIP treatment," said Lulu, sliding into the booth. "How fancy."

"Only the best for my friends," said Sonya.

"This place is packed," I said as an entire baseball team streamed in through the front door, cleats still on and shirts untucked, with mud streaked on most of their pants.

"Yeah, it's a good sign, huh?" said Sonya. "I'm so excited for my mom. She's wanted to open a place like this forever."

Just then Ricki walked up to us while carefully balancing a gorgeous pie on a shiny silver tray. "Hi, everyone. This is fresh out of the oven. Who'd like the first slice?" she asked.

Just looking at the pie—the flaky brown crust, the bright, sweet-looking strawberries bursting out of the top—made my mouth water.

And since no one else spoke up, I said, "I'll have it."

Sonya's mom set the platter down with a wink. "Please be my guest—and be honest: this is a new recipe, and I'd love to get your opinion." She placed a slice on a plate and set it down in front of me.

I took a generous forkful, raised it to my lips, bit down, and almost choked.

Ricki cringed. "Oh, dear. I didn't mean *that* honest."

I tried to smile politely as I spit the crust out into my napkin. Except it's hard to be polite while spitting. Especially while spitting out baked goods directly in front of the actual baker.

Sonya must've thought I was kidding around, because she snapped, "That's not funny, Maggie. Someone might see you."

"I know, and I'm sorry," I said, looking around the shop. Luckily, no one seemed to be paying attention to our table. "But there's something wrong with that pie. It tastes like the ocean at Coney Island."

"Like medical waste?" asked Milo.

I elbowed him and clarified. "No, like salt."

Finn pulled the pie closer to him, took a tiny slice of crust, and set it on the tip of his tongue.

Immediately, his face twisted into an expression of disgust as he fought his gag reflex. "She's right," he said with a cough. "It's nasty."

Sonya tasted the pie, too, and spit it out fast. "Mom," she whispered. "We've got a big problem."

Ricki sat down at the booth and took a forkful for herself. After chewing and forcing herself to swallow, she said, "Blech. Something went horribly wrong. Let me have that." She whisked the pie away from us as though it were a ticking time bomb.

"The shakes are delicious, I swear," said Sonya. "Especially the chocolate banana. Can I get you one on the house?"

"Yuck," I said, crinkling my nose.

"But you love chocolate and bananas," said Sonya.

"I love chocolate and bananas on their own, but not mixed together," I explained.

"You are so weird," Lulu said.

"I feel the same way," said Finn.

"That your sister is a weirdo?" asked Lulu.

"No, that banana-flavored anything is disgusting," said Finn.

"Thank you." My brother and I high-fived across the table. Lulu and Milo looked at each other and shook their heads, like they thought they were both dating the craziest kids in town. I felt like I was starring in some corny teen movie. And that wasn't a bad thing.

"What about other fruit, like strawberries or raspberries?" Sonya asked.

"They're great on their own, but I don't understand why it's necessary to put them in other stuff," I said.

Sonya cracked up. "Know what? I'm going to make you the best shake you've ever had."

"What are you putting in it?" I asked.

"I'll surprise you," she said, heading back to the counter.

I got up and followed her.

"Afraid I'm gonna try to sneak some fruit into your milk shake?" Sonya asked.

"No, I just want to see how it's done," I said.

Sonya stepped behind the counter while I hopped onto a stool.

"This is my cousin Felicity," Sonya said. "Felicity, this is Maggie Brooklyn. Will you make her a chocolate malted?"

"And hold the banana," I added.

"Sure, boss. Coming right up," said Felicity as she poured milk, chocolate syrup, ice cream, and malted powder into a high-tech blender.

As soon as she punched the ON button the machine whirred to life, pulverizing that sugary goodness like there was no tomorrow.

The loud *whirr* got louder, and suddenly something flew through the air. Next, I felt a cold, wet sensation on my face. I gasped as something icy dripped down my chin.

It took a moment to process this new, freezing-wet reality. I had milk shake in my hair and milk shake in my ears. Milk shake stuck to my eyelashes and dripped off the tip of my nose.

"Blech!" I yelled, wiping the shake out of my eyes.

Being drenched in chocolate shake doesn't sound like such a hardship, I realize. But trust me, it was bad—a soppy, sticky mess. And most definitely not the look I was going for this afternoon.

To think I'd spent so much time selecting my outfit—jeans that were perfectly worn in and a yellow V-neck shirt, buttery soft and fitted but not tight, plus my new brown leather jacket. At least my jacket was back at the table, but still—I was a mess.

"Oh, poor Maggie," Lulu said, handing me a large pile of napkins.

I wiped my face as best I could but still felt sticky, so I excused myself to head to the restroom.

It turned out even the bathroom had been designed to fit in with the vintage theme. Old-fashioned ads for soap and Coca-Cola lined the walls. The sink was pedestal-style, and the toilet had a chain flush. They'd really gone all out.

After I finished washing the remaining milk shake from my hair, I headed back to the booth. But before I made it there, I heard a horrible crash.

Glass shattered and people screamed.

Next came an eerie silence.

Time seemed to stop, but only momentarily. Suddenly Ricki raced to the front of the store, as if she was chasing someone. And through the hole in the picture window, I saw a person race away.

Wait. Something wasn't right. A hole in the picture window? I blinked and tried to process what was right in front of me.

The gorgeous picture window—the one Sonya's dad had worked so hard on—was shattered. Lying in the middle of the broken glass was a rectangular piece of cardboard. I tiptoed through the shards and picked it up, carefully, with my thumb and forefinger. It was a piece of cardboard box. Someone had written a message on it in block print.

Sonya noticed me and walked over.

"What's that?" she asked.

I handed her the note and explained, "I found this in the glass."

Sonya squinted at the note in confusion. "What does this mean?" she asked.

I looked from the shattered window to my friend. Then I took a deep breath before answering her. "I think someone's trying to sabotage the store."

I didn't say what else I was thinking, which was this: looks like I've got a new mystery to solve.

# Chapter 2

◆ ◆ ◆

I should probably explain a few things now. My name is Maggie Brooklyn, and I am not your typical seventh grader.

Wait, let me start over.

That makes me sound kind of snobby, or like a wannabe superhero. And I'm not a snob or a wannabe superhero. Being a superhero would be cool; believe me, if someone offered me magical powers, I wouldn't turn them down. I'd love to fly or make myself invisible or have X-ray vision like those machines they have in all the airports now. But no one's given me the option. I am a mere mortal, and not only that—I'm actually extremely typical in a lot of ways. If "typical" can be described as an extreme state of being.

I'm not sure.

Anyway, I'm a little over five feet tall, with wavy

brown hair and greenish-brownish eyes and parents who are way too strict. Oh, and I have a twin brother named Finn, but that's probably obvious by now.

I'm in seventh grade and not super popular, but not unpopular, either.

I have an after-school job walking a few neighborhood dogs. And lately, as I've been walking my dogs, I've also been walking into a mystery or three.

It's funny; the more mysteries I find and solve, the more mysteries seem to find me. And today was no exception. Between the salty pie, the shattered glass, the threatening note, and the flying milk shake, one thing was obvious: Sonya's Sweets was in trouble.

But did these problems amount to what usually happened with the opening of a new store? Or was something sinister going on?

Inquiring minds—at least *my* inquiring mind—needed to know.

But first things first. Ricki quickly determined that having shards of glass and a gaping hole in her store was potentially dangerous, and most certainly bad for business, so she shuffled everyone out and closed up shop.

Everyone, that is, except for us; Sonya convinced her to let me, Milo, Finn, and Lulu stick around to help out.

Once the store had been cleared of customers, I

showed Sonya's mom the note. I realized, now that things had calmed down a bit, that the message was printed on the back of a box of Girl Scout cookies. Thin Mints—my favorite. Of course, Thin Mints are everybody's favorite, right?

"Where did you find this?" Ricki asked, looking from the words on the box up to me and then back again, as if she couldn't believe her eyes.

"Right in the middle of the glass," I said. "Like an angry message from the outside."

As Ricki stared at the note, her brow furrowed. "Sit tight, everyone. I need to call the police before I clean up this mess."

"Can we help?" Lulu asked.

"You can help by staying where you are. I don't want anyone getting hurt."

After Ricki went to the back, the rest of us sat there in silence.

Poor Sonya looked about ready to cry. I wanted to say something to make her feel better. I just didn't know what that something might be.

Just then I heard laughter from behind me. I spun around. Felicity was giggling with Joshua behind the counter. He snapped a damp dish towel at her, and she laughed even harder.

The two of them seemed oblivious to the mess,

which struck me as odd. Because, this shattered window thing? It seemed like a very big deal.

Once Felicity noticed me staring, her smile faded. She turned away from Joshua and began wiping down the counter.

Sonya shook her head. "I cannot believe this is happening. It's like the best day of my life and the worst day of my life, all wrapped into one."

"Well, at least it was fun while it lasted," said Lulu.

"And it's not over. Everything's going to be okay. I'm sure this is just some random fluke," I said, wishing I could make myself sound more convincing.

"What do you mean?" asked Sonya. "You just said you think someone is trying to sabotage the store."

"Right," I said weakly. "But 'think' is the key word. None of us should jump to conclusions. It's too soon to know anything, really."

When Ricki joined us a minute later, I could tell by the look on her face that her call to the police had not gone well.

"What did they say?" asked Sonya. "Are we in danger? Should we shut down? Will I have to change my name? Because what if there's a crazy person trying to destroy anything and anyone with the name Sonya?"

Ricki rubbed Sonya's back. "One question at a time,

sweetie. Let's not panic. I don't think one broken window means we're in life-threatening danger."

"But what about the note?" asked Sonya.

"I can't explain the note," said Ricki. "But the police seem to think it's a prank. And maybe they're right. Perhaps I overreacted, closing up the shop so fast."

I looked around the near-empty store.

Some of the chairs had been knocked over in people's haste to get out. Chocolate milk shake still dripped from the wall behind where I'd been standing. The place seemed to be a huge mess of dirty plates and cookie crumbs—an ugly scene.

It occurred to me that in her rush to clear out Sonya's Sweets, Ricki hadn't actually waited for people to pay their bills. That meant she'd given away all her food for free.

"What a horrible way to end a grand opening," said Ricki. "This is pretty much the opposite of grand. I'd say it's been one big failure." I saw tears well up in Ricki's eyes, but she blinked them back in her struggle to put on a brave face.

It's hard seeing your friend's mom so upset. I wanted to offer up words of encouragement, but I couldn't think of a way to put a positive spin on things.

Still, I had to do something, so I pulled Ricki aside and said, "Something tells me this is more than a simple prank. I'm going to look into it."

"Thanks, Maggie." Ricki smiled at me weakly. Her expression told me she didn't have much faith, probably because I'm just a kid. I understood why she felt this way.

I just hoped I'd be able to prove her wrong.

Soon.

# Chapter 3

◆ ◆ ◆

"What now?" asked Milo once the four of us had spilled out onto the sidewalk.

"I need to go home and do some serious homework," said Finn, checking his watch. "If I don't finish before dark, my mom won't let me go out tonight."

"I'll come, too," said Lulu. "I still have to write that English paper for Mr. Dean."

"You guys didn't finish yet?" I asked.

"Of course not. It's only Saturday. What kind of nerd finishes their homework before Saturday?" asked Finn.

"No comment," I said, turning red.

"I did my homework, too," said Milo.

"Really?" asked Lulu. "Or are you just trying to make Maggie feel better?"

"Well, I did most of my homework." Milo shrugged

his skinny shoulders. "I'm lucky because my grandma doesn't care when I do it, as long as it gets done. I'll probably finish Sunday night. That's what I usually do."

"You and most people," said Finn. "Hey, where did you put your homework, Maggie?"

"Why do you ask?" I feigned innocence even though I knew exactly where Finn was going with this line of questioning.

I knew not because we're twins and we can read each other's minds—we can't. Or at least I can't read Finn's mind, and if he can read mine, he's not telling me. I knew because Finn always tries to copy my homework. This has been going on ever since we started getting homework, in kindergarten or whenever; I can't even remember. That's how far back it goes.

"Nice try," I said. "But you're not copying."

"I never said I wanted to copy," said Finn. "I just want to check my answers against yours once I'm finished—make sure you didn't make any mistakes."

"Don't sweat it," said Lulu, grabbing Finn's hand. "I know all of her hiding spots."

"Cool. I knew there was a reason I hung out with you," said Finn.

I shot Lulu a dirty look, but she winked and giggled.

"You were my friend first!" I told her, only half in jest.

"Don't worry," she called as she pulled my brother away. "We're not going to steal your precious answers."

And before I could say another word they took off down the street, leaving me and Milo in the dust.

Milo cleared his throat and brushed his floppy bangs off his forehead. Tried to, anyway. They flopped right back down, as usual. "I'm heading over to Southpaw to check out this month's concert schedule. Want to come?"

"Sure," I said. "If we can stop for frozen yogurt on the way. I never got my dessert fix."

"Sure you did," said Finn. "You got it right in the face."

"Ugh, don't remind me." I ran my fingers through my still-sticky hair and tried not to think about the giant brown stain on my shirt. At least my leather jacket covered it up, for the most part.

"Chocolate malted is the best perfume around," said Milo. "So, where are we heading? Wait—Culture, right? I shouldn't even bother asking."

I grinned; Milo knows me so well. Or at least he knows my taste in frozen yogurt. Culture serves the best in Brooklyn, and they've got the lines to prove it. Seriously—half our school eats lunch there. Last time I went, I waited so long I barely had time to finish before I had to head back to class. And in case you were wondering, brain freeze from frozen yogurt is just as painful as the ice cream variety.

Milo and I headed straight for Culture, where we joined the line. It was humongous. Even today, on this chilly "keep-your-jacket-zipped-all-the-way-up" Saturday, we waited for half an hour. But the waiting is worth it, because their plain tart yogurt with miniature dark chocolate chips is awesome. Regular chocolate chips aren't anything special, but something about having them in miniature makes them so much better.

It's the texture, I suppose.

I explained this to Milo as we strolled toward Southpaw, a cool and grungy concert hall. It's a twenty-minute walk, but I didn't mind, because walking helps me think. And today I had plenty to think about.

What was going on at Sonya's Sweets? Who would shatter that window or write that note? Why were Felicity and Joshua laughing when things were so obviously bad? Did they know something the rest of us didn't? Could the two of them have anything to do with the note? Or were they simply wrapped up in their own joke?

I needed to investigate, gather evidence, the works. It was just that today, for some reason, I wasn't sure where to begin.

When we were about halfway to Southpaw, Milo asked, "You okay?"

I guess I'd been pretty quiet. "Sure. I'm just trying to sort things out."

"You mean about the whole broken window?"

"Well, yeah, and not just that." I kicked a stone and watched it bounce into the gutter. "That note was so creepy. 'Take your cookies elsewhere'? Who would write that?"

"What if the police were right and it's all someone's weird idea of a joke?" said Milo.

"That sounds sort of like a cop-out to me," I said.

"Then maybe it was a Girl Scout," he said.

I laughed.

"I'm serious," said Milo. "The note *was* written on the back of a Girl Scout cookie box. So think about it: some evil zombie Girl Scout attacks the ice cream parlor. What could be more simple? This case is closed. You're done!"

I grinned up at Milo and asked, "Why zombies?"

"Zombies are trendy," Milo said matter-of-factly. "Aren't they?"

I shrugged. "I guess so. But don't you think a Girl Scout—either zombie or mortal—wouldn't be so obvious about her crime? Wouldn't she try to use regular paper, at least?"

"You have a good point," said Milo. "And I'm sure you'll figure it all out. You always do."

"Yeah, but usually I start with some sort of clue."

"What about the note?"

"Sonya's mom has it," I said.

"But I'll bet you've memorized the words, the color of the ink, the size of the paper, and everything else about it."

"True," I said with a nod. "And it's cardboard, not paper, remember? And the writing was extra neat. It was written in pale blue, like the kind of ink that comes from a highlighter, not a regular marker. Probably a wide tip, but perhaps regular size. Definitely not a fine point. Plus, the note had tape at the top of it. Except it wasn't just taped to the window, obviously."

"Maybe someone taped it to a rock and then threw it in."

"That makes sense," I said. "Except I didn't see a rock. The box was just lying there. But now that you mention it, I actually have no idea what broke that window. I should've looked harder."

"We all looked, and we couldn't find a thing," Milo reminded me.

"Which is almost a clue in itself," I said, thinking out loud. "How did it disappear so quickly? Maybe someone from inside the shop took it with them."

Milo thought about this for a few moments. "Maybe. I'm sure you'll figure it out. You're a natural."

"I don't think I am," I replied.

"Don't put yourself down," said Milo. "That's just crazy."

"No, that's not what I mean. I know I'm good at solving mysteries, but it's not because I'm talented. I think I'm good because it's something I like doing. And the more mysteries I solve, the easier it gets, because solving mysteries is simply what I choose to devote my time to. It's all about focus and hard work and concentration. My dad always says the question you should ask yourself shouldn't be, 'What are you good at?' it's 'What do you *want* to be good at?' And 'How can you make yourself good?' "

Milo nodded. "I know what you mean. It's the same thing with me and my chess game. I used to be lousy, but I didn't care. When my mom first taught me how to play, I thought it was the most boring game in the world."

"So what changed?" I asked.

"She got sick, and I had to play the game with her, because it was all she had the strength to do."

"Oh." I never know exactly what to say when Milo talks about his mom. She died a few years ago, before I knew him.

"Chessboards are easy to bring to the hospital," he said. "Also, you can start and stop, interrupt a game at any moment, then pick up and play days or even weeks later. That's what we had to do when my mom was getting her treatments. Sometimes she was too weak to play. But she always came back to it."

Milo stopped talking, and I felt like I should respond, except I didn't know how to. "She sounds amazing," I said quietly, awkwardly.

"I don't know," said Milo. "She was my mom. She was cool, for the most part. I mostly just remember the good stuff. Her curly hair, and how it always smelled like coconut. Which, it turned out, was from her shampoo."

Even though Milo was standing right next to me, his voice sounded a million miles away. "She loved chess. And it wasn't until she was gone that I really got into it. It's almost like I wanted to be good for her. Even though she's not around anymore. I feel closer to her when I'm playing."

"That's beautiful," I said.

Milo laughed, embarrassed. "Whatever."

Afraid of saying the wrong thing, I stayed quiet. I don't know that many details about Milo's mom's death; just that she was sick for a while and then she died and left him and his dad alone—except Milo lives with his grandma now. His dad is in Brooklyn, too, but in another part of the borough. The two of them don't get along so well. Milo's grandma is sweet, and she's not even old, by grandma standards. Her hair is brown and everything—not white. And she bicycles all over town.

She's his mom's mom, and I wondered if they looked alike, whether his mom liked biking everywhere, too. I wanted to know more about Milo's mom, but I didn't want to ask because it seemed rude, somehow, or at least uncomfortable.

So we walked in silence for the rest of the way, and when we got to Southpaw, Milo picked up two schedules and handed one to me. Scanning it, he frowned. "Everything I want to see starts after my curfew. It totally blows."

"How come concerts have to start so late?" I asked.

"Don't know." Milo crumpled the schedule and tossed it in the trash. Then he bent down to pet a passing poodle that promptly bared his pointy white teeth and growled.

"Sorry," said the owner—a hipster in skinny jeans with a tattoo of a dragon on his neck and a bowler hat on his head. "He's kind of a jerk sometimes. Don't take it personally."

"I won't," Milo replied, standing up straight again.

The jerky poodle reminded me of something, but I couldn't remember what. Oh, wait—that's it. Dog walking! "I've got to walk Nofarm this afternoon!" I said.

"But it's Saturday," said Milo. "Don't you take weekends off?"

"Usually, but Nofarm's family just moved, so they asked me for this special favor."

"What time are you supposed to be there?" Milo asked.

I checked my watch. "Ten minutes ago."

"Let's go," he said.

Milo and I sprinted all the way to Eighth Avenue and Carroll Street—an uphill journey, I'd like to note.

Once there, I bent over and tried to catch my breath. "Tried" being the key word in that last sentence. I was huffing and puffing, sweat pooled in the small of my back, and my legs felt achy from sprinting. I gazed up at the building. Nofarm's family had moved to a fifth-floor walk-up, and I wasn't yet ready for the steps.

Milo didn't seem to be, either: his hands were also on his knees. He squinted at Nofarm's new place—a beautiful but run-down old mansion made of large red bricks. The staircase leading to the oversize double front doors was wide and sweeping. Three tall spires met up at the top to form the roof. They were super pointy, as if poking the blue sky above.

"This is where they live?" he asked.

"Not in the whole building," I said. "It's a bunch of apartments now." I walked toward the front steps and started to climb.

"Hold on!" said Milo. "Do you know what this place is?"

I turned around to face him, wondering why he hadn't moved. "I just told you," I said. "It's Nofarm's family's new building. Are you coming, or would you rather wait for me down here?"

"Neither," said Milo, gazing up at the place with dread.

"Why not?" I asked.

"Because that's not only Nofarm's new building," Milo said, "it's Brooklyn's most famous haunted mansion."

# Chapter 4

◆ ◆ ◆

I laughed in his face. I mean, obviously I laughed, because I couldn't fathom that Milo was serious. Haunted mansions? Who believed in haunted mansions? And if this mansion was so famous, how come I'd never heard of it before? I've lived in Park Slope for my whole life. This building has been here for a lot longer than that. And never, ever, do I recall hearing anyone mention anything about it being haunted, which I told Milo in between fits of laughter.

"You don't know what you're talking about, Maggie," he said, his tone harsher than I'd ever heard it before. I guess he was still reeling from being laughed at.

I tried to stop. It wasn't easy.

"Okay, it's haunted," I said, deciding to humor him. "But how can you say it's famous when I've never even heard of it?"

Milo frowned and shook his head, unable to speak.

Did I mention that my boyfriend is kind of sensitive? And when I say "kind of," I actually mean "very."

"This mansion used to belong to the Adams family," he said.

"The what family?" I asked, walking back to where he stood on the sidewalk.

"You've heard of Jonas Adams, right? He's the guy who invented Adams miniature chocolate bars."

"Never heard of him, but I love Adams Chocolate," I replied.

"Of course you do," said Milo. "Everyone loves Adams Chocolate. They're more famous than Hershey and Cadbury put together, and their classic mini bar is insanely delicious. Those first bites are so sweet and satisfying. Even the sound of them tumbling out of the cardboard box is pleasing."

"You sound like a commercial," I told him.

"Yeah, because I really like the chocolate. You didn't know it was invented here in Brooklyn? Their old factory was right next door. It's condos now." Milo pointed to a familiar looking high-rise.

"My friend Beatrix lives there," I said. "On the top floor."

"That's where they made all of their chocolate-flavored bubble gum, which was really popular about a hundred years ago."

"I had no idea you were such a chocolate historian, Milo."

"It's part of Brooklyn's history," Milo replied, not realizing I was teasing him. "The chocolate gum was huge."

"So you're telling me this old mansion is haunted by a bubble-gum inventor?" I asked.

"Not exactly—"

"What's the problem?" I asked, interrupting. "He died and continued to stick around?"

I fake laughed at my own joke. One of us had to! Milo insisted on staring at me in silence, almost like he was annoyed. But that made no sense. It's not like I did anything wrong.

I elbowed him and forced myself to smile, even though his expression made me nervous. "It's a joke. Get it? He stuck around? Because gum is sticky?"

"I get it," Milo grumbled.

"Okay, clearly that wasn't my best material, but what is wrong with you?" I asked.

"If you knew the real story, you wouldn't be laughing." Milo blinked up at the building and shivered. Then he lowered his voice, almost like he was scared that these alleged ghosts were listening. "This whole mansion used to belong to the Adams family. It's the biggest place in the entire neighborhood. The family was so loaded. There's an elevator inside; their house was the first to have a private elevator in all of Brooklyn."

"It's still pretty rare, I'd think. Right?" I asked. "I don't know anyone with their own elevator."

"Neither do I," said Milo. "Anyway, one summer the Adams family went to their summerhouse in Maine, and one of their servants stayed behind. The maid. I guess she was supposed to take care of the place. Except the elevator broke and she got stuck inside, and no one knew."

"Yikes."

"They didn't find her for an entire month."

"Double yikes. She must've been starving," I said.

Milo shook his head. "She was way worse than starving, Maggie. She was dead."

"Oh." Suddenly the wind picked up and seemed to blow right through my jacket. I shivered. "That's awful."

"I know. They don't even know if she starved to death or suffocated first. I don't think there was much air circulation in those old elevators. Really, it was just one giant coffin."

I felt both creeped out and skeptical at the very same time. "Are you sure this story is true?" I asked.

"That's what I heard," said Milo. "The maid's name was Margaret, and she still haunts the place, apparently. People hear her singing, and she moves stuff around. My grandma knows someone who used to live there, and they had to move away because she used to visit them every night."

"Visit them?" I asked. "Like, in their sleep?"

Milo nodded.

"Doesn't that mean they had nightmares? That they imagined the whole thing?"

"No, there was physical evidence, too. Their glasses kept breaking."

I kept waiting for Milo to smile, to laugh and tell me he was kidding, except he didn't.

"What do you mean, their glasses kept breaking?" I asked.

"Just what I told you," Milo replied stubbornly.

"Drinking glasses or eyeglasses?" I wondered.

"Stop making fun of me," Milo said.

"I'm not making fun of you. I'm making fun of the idea of ghosts."

"Same thing," Milo claimed.

It wasn't, but I decided not to harp on the issue. "So you honestly believe that this place is haunted?"

"Yup," Milo replied.

I tilted my head, trying to figure out how to break the news to him gently. "But Milo, there's no such thing as ghosts."

"How do you know?"

"I just do."

"Do you have proof?" he asked.

I laughed, but his expression remained stoic.

I tried again. "I don't have proof there aren't ghosts, but I don't have proof there are, either. I always figured ghosts are like unicorns or the tooth fairy: something you believe in as a kid, and then grow out of."

"So you're calling me a kid now?" asked Milo. "I'm three months and two days older than you. And Margaret was a real person. My grandma showed me an article about the accident. She was from Ireland, and had just moved to New York to make money for her family."

"That doesn't make any sense," I said.

"Lots of immigrants came over from Ireland back then," said Milo. "Look it up. That's where my great-grandparents came from. Park Slope was full of people like them."

"That's not what I mean," I said. "There's no way that Margaret's ghost is haunting the place. Because there's no such thing as ghosts."

"Haven't you ever seen or heard something you couldn't explain?" Milo asked. "Don't you ever get the feeling that someone's watching you?"

"Sure," I said. "But that doesn't mean those sensations are caused by ghosts."

"Well, it doesn't mean they aren't."

Milo's eyes, which were normally super warm and sweet—twinkly, even—got dark and kind of squinty.

He balled his fists together, as if he felt his anger so intensely he couldn't contain it.

I'd never seen him so upset before, and it made me uneasy. I giggled out of nervousness, but this seemed to anger him more.

"If you're just going to make fun of me, I'm not going to stick around," he said gruffly.

"Wait," I said. "Are you really upset? I didn't mean to hurt your feelings."

"You didn't," said Milo, clearly wounded. "But I've gotta go."

Before I got the chance to ask him what was going on, he took off. And I couldn't even chase after him, because I had to get to work.

I watched Milo walk up Eighth Avenue and turn right onto First Street, out of sight. Then I took one last look up at the mansion from the sidewalk. It was kind of spooky-looking—large and imposing, and the twisty, dead tree out front didn't help matters one bit, but that didn't mean a thing. It was just a building. I knew this for a fact.

So, after taking a deep breath, I bounded up the stairs to the front door and rang the buzzer.

"Who is it?" one of Beckett's moms asked.

"It's me, Maggie," I said.

The lock clicked, and I hauled the heavy door open

and bounded up an old, creaky staircase, all the way to the fifth floor. Then I knocked on the door to apartment 5A.

Nofarm, a super-friendly, supersized, and scrappy mutt bounded toward me as soon as the door opened.

Caroline greeted me, too. She's tall, with long, red, curly hair, and wore black leggings, a baggy white sweater, and no shoes. Her toenails were painted dark, dark red. The rest of her family—her wife, Lisa, and their son, Beckett—must've been out, because I couldn't hear anyone else in the house.

"Down, boy," I said, scratching Nofarm behind his ears and trying to get him to calm down. Or at least get him off of me.

"No jumping, Nofarm," said Caroline. "Down, boy! Sorry, Maggie. Please come in." Caroline gestured toward the messy living room. "Welcome to our new home!"

I stepped inside and surveyed the scene. The place was filled with boxes. Most were empty, but some were still full and stacked taller than me. Crumpled newspaper littered the floor. And those Styrofoam peanut things were everywhere.

"I like the new place." I said this to be polite, but actually I couldn't tell whether I liked their place or not. The living room was such a mess, I had to stretch my imagination. The apartment had the potential to be lovely, though. It was on the fifth floor, which meant it rose above the treetops and faced the park, which I could see from the large windows in back.

"Wait until we're actually set up," said Caroline. "Of course, you may have to wait a while. I can't believe how hard this move has been."

"I'm sure," I said. "Let me know if I can help."

"Oh, you're helping by walking Nofarm. Believe me. But since you mentioned it, we could use another favor. How do you feel about babysitting?"

"I love it!" I said. "Wait—I should be more accurate. I *assume* I will love it, but I don't know for sure because I've never done it before. But Finn and I—Finn is my twin brother—just took a babysitting safety class at the local hospital."

"Impressive," Caroline said with a nod. "You've actually studied up on babysitting. I didn't even know that was possible."

I shrugged. "It was my mom's idea, actually. She's like that—always thinking ahead, planning, and signing us up for stuff. She's not so into us having downtime."

It's true, too. If my mom finds out we have nothing to do on a Saturday, she has this amazing ability to find an Indian cooking class, a Claymation workshop, or an origami-folding lesson nearby. And if all else fails, she'll volunteer us to sort through clothes at the Salvation Army. Except last month the Salvation Army warehouse had a bedbug scare, so that's why she signed us up for the babysitting preparation course at the local hospital instead.

"So, you are willing? To babysit, I mean?" asked Caroline. "Because it's our anniversary next Saturday night, and we're really in a bind."

"Yes, definitely. Wait—you do mean babysit for Beckett, right?"

Caroline smiled and raised her eyebrows. "He is our only child, for the time being."

"Right. I knew that. Just clarifying," I said. Beckett, Lisa and Caroline's son, is cute, but kind of a handful. And when I say "kind of," I actually mean "really." Last week Beckett's moms had to take him to the emergency room because he told them he swallowed a nail. It turned out he did it on purpose: he wanted to know what it would feel like going down.

It felt painful, apparently. They told me he bawled for the entire taxi ride to the emergency room. But luckily for him, there was no permanent damage, because Beckett hadn't swallowed a nail—he'd swallowed a small garden snail. His moms had misheard him.

The doctor seemed less alarmed about the snail. It would pass naturally, he told them. And it did. Not that

I have physical evidence—I don't need it. That's the kind of thing I'd rather take their word for.

The more I thought about it, the more I realized babysitting for Beckett could be fairly complicated.

On the other hand, what else was I going to do on Saturday night? There was nothing good on TV that I could recall. "Sure, I'd love to," I said.

"Oh, that's fantastic, Maggie. Thank you. We're having some issues with our regular sitter."

"Issues?" I couldn't help but ask.

Caroline rolled her eyes. "Yup; ever since the move. She's a little superstitious. In fact, she won't even set foot in this building. Once she found out where we'd moved, she quit via text message."

"Is it because of that old ghost story?" I asked.

"You've heard about it, too?" asked Caroline.

"Yup. Just now. My boyfriend, Milo, told me about it right before I showed up." I didn't mention that we'd also kind of fought about it and Milo had stormed off. That seemed like too much information, although it was on my mind.

"Did you hear that she cleans? The ghost, I mean. She was a maid from Ireland. Margaret was her name, and apparently she still dusts."

"Milo didn't go into any details," I said. "I did know her name was Margaret."

"Isn't that your name, too?" asked Caroline.

"Technically," I said. "But no one calls me that. I've been Maggie forever."

"I told Lisa, if the ghost maid cleans, she can stay as long as she wants. That's exactly what—"

Caroline was interrupted by a loud booming sound and the shattering of glass.

"What was that?" Caroline asked, hurrying to the back of the apartment.

I followed her to the master bedroom, where both of us froze and stared at each other in shock.

A giant mirror lay in the middle of the room, like it had face-planted there. Razor-sharp pieces of glass were everywhere.

"Unbelievable!" said Caroline. "That was my favorite piece of furniture."

"How'd that happen, do you think?" I wondered.

Caroline shrugged. "It was propped up on the wall, and I guess it wasn't that secure. The wind must've knocked it down."

This explanation made sense; it *was* kind of windy outside. But here's the weird thing: when I glanced at the wall of windows on the other side of the room, I couldn't help but notice that every single one of them was closed.

# Chapter 5

◆ ◆ ◆

"I'd better walk Nofarm now," I said, backing out of the room. I felt overcome with a strange sensation—a sort of suffocating nervousness, and an overwhelming desire to leave.

"Good idea. He's been acting so strange ever since the move," Caroline said, turning away from the mess and toward Nofarm, who stared at us from just outside the bedroom door.

"What do you mean, 'strange'?" I asked.

"Well, sometimes I hear him whimpering in his sleep, and when he's awake he'll often pace back and forth across the living room. Other times, he scratches at the walls like he's trying to dig his way out."

"And he never acted like that before?" I asked.

"Nope," Caroline said, with the shake of her head. "I don't know what his problem is."

"Dogs are extremely sensitive," I told her. "They have amazing hearing, and their sense of smell is insane. That's why so many of them are trained for service—you know, for the blind or the police. People who get seizures and panic attacks sometimes use them, because service dogs are so perceptive they can often prevent episodes."

"Well, Nofarm is just a scrappy mutt. Right, guy?" She scratched his back, and he wagged his tail like crazy.

"Maybe he needs to get used to the building," I said.

"That makes sense," said Caroline. "And he's not the only one."

"I guess we should get going," I said as I tugged gently on Nofarm's leash. He acted super enthusiastic about leaving.

Nofarm and I raced down the steps, taking the last flight two at a time. As soon as I burst through the heavy door to the outside, I felt better.

Nofarm did, too, it seemed. The scrappy little mutt was back to his usual perky self. I could tell because he was in typical happy-dog pose—tail high and wagging, eyes forward, mouth open in a loud, panting doggie smile.

We went all the way to the picnic house in Prospect Park, walking past three soccer games being played simultaneously in the Long Meadow.

On the sidelines, I noticed two sets of twins playing catch with their moms.

As usual, lots and lots of dogs roamed around—giant dogs and tiny dogs and everything in between, mutts and purebreds alike. Most dogs in Brooklyn, regardless of their kind, eventually make their way to Prospect Park. It's a glorious place for all creatures.

Things were particularly busy this Saturday, probably because the weather was so lovely. Most dogs strolled with their owners, but I did run into Jane, another neighborhood dog walker I happen to know.

"You're working weekends now?" she asked, adjusting her chunky, square-ish glasses. Jane's dark hair was shorter now—it came up past her shoulders, and she was wearing her usual outfit: dark jeans and a red hoodie.

"Just today," I said.

"Good. I don't need any more competition." She said it as though she was kidding, but it's hard to tell with Jane. She's a full-time dog walker, and super competitive about it. She's eccentric, which I suppose is a more polite way of saying she's odd. Jane is often blunt and paranoid, and sometimes she comes across as a jerk. But I've noticed that even jerky people usually have something going for them, if you dig deep enough, and Jane is no exception. Her secret superpower is being amazing with dogs.

She was currently on her knees, scratching Nofarm's neck with both hands. And Nofarm was digging it, I could tell. His tail thumped hard on the pavement. His chin was raised high, and he licked her occasionally as if to say, "Keep it up, babe."

Jane laughed and squinted up at me. "Nofarm is such a cutie. Can I give him a treat?" she asked.

"Sure, as long as it's just one," I said. "He gets so much food from Beckett. The kid is only three, but he's clever. He's already figured out how to get rid of all his vegetables, so his moms are really strict about his diet. The dog's diet, I mean. Beckett seems to get whatever he wants."

Jane made Nofarm sit and shake, and she tried to get him to roll over.

"I think that's too advanced for the little guy," I said.

"Oh, Maggie. I've taught all the dogs I walk how to roll over. It's kind of basic." Jane pulled a treat out of her pocket and handed it over. Nofarm chomped it down, fast.

"Good boy," Jane said, patting his head.

"So, how's it going?" I asked.

"Can't complain," said Jane. "Well, not yet, anyway. Once winter comes and I'm trekking through snow and sleet, then I'll complain plenty."

"I can't wait!" I said.

Jane looked at me, all confused. Did I mention she has no sense of humor?

Jane has no sense of humor.

"No," she went on. "You won't be able to stand it. I'll bet that's when you'll turn in your leashes."

"Huh?" I asked.

"Retire from dog walking," she explained. "Just be sure to refer all of your old clients to me. Deal?"

"Hey, who are you with today?" I asked, pointing to the two chocolate Labs by Jane's side. Changing the subject seemed like a good idea, and I was curious, too.

"Flower Power and Skittles," Jane replied.

"Which is which?" I asked.

Jane smiled down at the dogs. "To be honest, I can't really tell. They look pretty identical. One thing's for sure, though: if you get a dog, you shouldn't let your five-year-old name it. I warned them not to, but do you think they listened? No way."

"Wait, you criticized your clients' kid's dog name ideas?" I asked.

"Of course I did," said Jane, with a completely straight face. "I feel like it's part of my job. Otherwise this park is going to be overrun by Scouts and Spots."

I laughed.

"You think that's funny? Listen to this: there are three dogs named Brooklyn in this neighborhood alone."

"That's funny, because Brooklyn is my middle name."

Jane cracked up. "That's a good one, Maggie."

"I'm serious," I said.

"Oh," said Jane. She faked a cough to hide her smirk. "I didn't realize your parents were weirdos."

"They're not," I said.

"That's what you think," Jane mumbled under her breath.

"Hey, can I ask you something? Have you lived here long?"

"In Park Slope?" asked Jane. "Oh, ten years or so. Is that long or short?"

"Long, I think," I said. "Have you ever heard of the Jonas Adams mansion at Eighth Avenue and Carroll Street?"

"The haunted mansion?" asked Jane, lowering her voice. "Of course I have. Why?"

"Because Nofarm's family just moved into the building," I explained.

"And you're still willing to walk him? Are you sure that's a good idea?" she asked as she stood up and tugged on Skittles's and Flower Power's leashes. "I should be going."

"Wait," I said. "Why do you say that?"

But it was too late. Jane was already hurrying away. "Can't hear you," she called, waving. "Good luck."

I guess Milo wasn't the only superstitious person

around. I picked up a stick and threw it to Nofarm, who played fetch for about ten minutes. When he grew tired, we continued on our way. And that's when I spotted someone who looked exactly like my friend Beatrix, speeding by on a bicycle.

I met Beatrix pretty recently, since she only just moved to Brooklyn from Manhattan at the beginning of the school year after her parents got divorced. Her dad still lives in the city, in their old apartment. But she and her mom are out here. Actually, they live in the high-rise at Eighth Avenue and Carroll Street, right next door to the haunted mansion.

And by "haunted mansion," what I really mean is, "Beckett's new building that's rumored to be haunted." Because there's no such thing as ghosts.

Obviously the shattered mirror was a strange and creepy coincidence.

Anyway, back to Beatrix. She's skinny with wild curly hair, which makes her look like a dandelion. In a good way, I mean. Beatrix is way pretty. Pretty enough to hang with the popular kids, if she wanted to, but she chooses to be friends with us instead. I thought Beatrix was in Manhattan today. That's where she told us she'd be. And it's why she couldn't make it to the Sonya's Sweets opening. Yet here she was in the neighborhood.

I waved, but she must not have seen me, because the closer she got, the more she sped up.

Then something really weird happened: when we were just a few feet apart, we made eye contact, but then she turned her head away.

"Hey, Beatrix!" I yelled as she rode by.

She skidded to a stop and turned around. "Oh, hi, Maggie. I didn't realize that was you." She hopped off her ten-speed and walked it over to where Nofarm and I were standing. "Which dog is this?" she asked.

"Nofarm Jones," I said. "Beckett's dog."

"He's a cutie," she said, bending down to pet him with her free hand.

"He lives next door to you, too," I said. "In that old mansion on the corner."

I watched Beatrix's reaction carefully. She didn't really seem to make any sort of connection, so she probably hadn't heard the rumors about ghosts. I found this comforting. But at the same time, it was annoying that I had to wonder so much about something that didn't even exist. Especially when I had more important things to worry about, like Sonya's Sweets.

"What are you doing in Brooklyn?" I asked.

"Um, I live here," said Beatrix. "Or at least I did last time I checked."

"I mean, I thought you were in Manhattan this

weekend. Isn't that why you couldn't come to the Sonya's Sweets opening?"

"Oh, yeah," said Beatrix. "I stayed at my dad's last night, but he had to work today so I came back early."

"Oh."

"He normally takes weekends off, but he's in the middle of some big project. I must've just missed you at Sonya's Sweets," she said.

"What do you mean?" I asked.

Beatrix checked her watch and then looked over her shoulder. "I stopped by, but Sonya wasn't there, either. It's a great place. Awesome desserts." Beatrix leaned her bike against her hip and pulled her hair into a high ponytail with both hands. It puffed out on top of her head, in full dandelion mode.

I didn't know what to say, because I didn't want to accuse my friend of lying. That's rude. Except the thing is, Beatrix was lying. And I couldn't pretend like she wasn't.

"Sonya's Sweets closed down early," I said. "You know—because of the window thing."

Beatrix's eyes got wide and her face blushed red. "Riiiight . . . ," she said. "Um, did I say I went in? I meant I walked by, and everything looked great. Obviously I didn't get to go in."

Beatrix's explanation didn't make much sense. But

what reason could she have to make stuff up? I couldn't figure it out.

"Why'd they have to close?" she asked.

I filled her in on the drama, then asked, "Didn't you notice the gaping hole in the window?"

Beatrix's brown eyes got even bigger than usual, and she stumbled over her words. "Um, yeah. Of course. I guess I got the address wrong and didn't realize that was the store. Do they have any idea how it happened?"

"Sonya's mom called the police, but they think it's just a prank, or an accident or something—nothing worth looking into, anyway."

"Think they're right?" she asked.

"I'm not sure," I said. "I'm still investigating."

"I'm sure you'll figure it out," said Beatrix. "But I've gotta run. See you at school Monday?"

"Sure," I said.

Beatrix hopped back onto her bicycle and pedaled off into the sunset, which made me realize that it must be getting late. "Let's go, Nofarm."

We were a half a block from Nofarm's new house when he stopped moving. I tugged on his leash but couldn't get him to budge, which struck me as odd, because Nofarm never acted this stubborn before. He's usually enthusiastic about walks but also excited to get home, because right after his afternoon walk he got his dinner.

Yet today, when he realized we were on our way home, he began to whimper. Then he laid down in the street and rested his chin on his paws. It was the same sad expression he'd worn in the new apartment.

"Come on!" I tried pulling again, but nothing worked. I had to carry him into the lobby, which wasn't easy. Did I mention Nofarm weighs fifty pounds?

No?

Nofarm weighs fifty pounds. He's squirmy, too. When I finally set him down, he sprinted up to his landing with his tail between his legs and his hair standing on end. He scratched at the door with his paw, as though he was desperate to get in. That's when I realized it wasn't the apartment that was making him nervous. It was the hallway.

Both Lisa and Caroline were in the living room when we returned. Lisa is shorter than Caroline and she has curly blond hair, just like Beckett's.

Beckett was nowhere in sight, but I heard some loud banging from the back of the apartment.

"Sorry about the noise," Lisa shouted. "That's Beckett with his new toy hammer."

"How was Nofarm tonight?" asked Caroline.

"He was amazing on the walk, but as soon as we headed back into the apartment building, he started freaking out. I actually had to carry him most of the way here."

Lisa looked at Caroline. “Yeah, I don’t know what’s up with him. His vet told us that adjusting to a new home might take time, but we had no idea he’d be this out of sorts!”

“It is weird,” I said.

We all watched Nofarm curl himself up into a ball in the back corner of the living room.

“I hear you’re babysitting on Saturday night,” said Lisa.

“Hopefully,” I replied. “I just need to ask my mom for permission. I’ll talk to her tonight and call you later, okay?”

Before she could answer me, Beckett raced across the living room screaming and waving a red plastic hammer, a pair of underwear on his head. “I hope those are clean,” Lisa yelled.

As I headed back downstairs I felt a sudden icy chill on my back. Also, I felt oddly short of breath. Not like I was suffocating, but almost. The ghost of Margaret is who I thought of, but I don’t know why because there’s no such thing as ghosts. Still, it all made me wonder—when it came to getting permission to babysit, did I want my mom to say yes, or no?

# Chapter 6

• • •

"It's no fair. How come you get all the jobs?" asked Finn. "Dog walking. Babysitting."

"You're allergic to dogs," I reminded him. "And the babysitting job just sprang organically from taking care of Nofarm."

"Still," said Finn. "I could totally use the cash. Oliver is working at the comic book store and Red gets paid to help his mom sell stuff on eBay, so I'm the only one of my friends who's always broke. I had to ask Mom for an advance on my allowance this week so I can go to the movies with Lulu."

"Hey, you asked me to borrow cash so you can go to that movie," I said.

"Right, because Mom said no. She's already advanced me two weeks' allowance. So according to her, I need to learn how to live within a budget."

"By borrowing money from your sister?" I asked.

"Exactly!" Finn grinned, and held out his hand for me to slap.

Obviously, I ignored it. "That smile probably works really well when you want something from Mom or Lulu, but I'm not buying it."

Even though I said this, I had to admit it was hard to stay mad at my brother. "How about I ask Lisa and Caroline to use us both next time?" I asked.

"That would be awesome," said Finn. "Thanks."

"Hey, have you ever heard of the Adams mansion on Eighth Avenue and Carroll Street?" I asked.

"Nope," said Finn. "How come?"

"That's where Beckett lives now. I went over there with Milo, and he had this whole story about some maid who died in the elevator who's haunting the place, and—"

"Wait—are you talking about the ghost at the chocolate mansion?" asked Finn.

"So you have heard of it?" I asked.

"Sure. I just didn't know where it was."

"Huh," I said. "What else do you know?"

"Nothing," said Finn. "Just that it's haunted. Red went there last Halloween and he swears he saw the ghost, but I don't believe him."

"Because ghosts don't exist, right?" I asked.

"Um, of course not," said Finn, looking at me carefully. "Are you okay, Mags?"

"Fine," I said, not really wanting to get into the whole story about my fight with Milo. If you can call it a fight; I'm still not sure. I flopped down on the couch next to my brother and changed the subject. "You'll love Beckett. The kid's hilarious."

"Hey, you did ask Mom for permission already, right?" asked Finn.

"Permission for what?" My mom asked as she walked into our room.

"How are you so good at sneaking up on us?" asked Finn.

"It's in the parent handbook," Mom said with a wink. "Right between chapters on how to tell when your kid is lying to you and methods of punishment."

"Funny," Finn said.

"What are you doing home so early?" I asked.

"My class got out early today," she replied.

My mom has recently taken up sculpting, because she's trying to get in touch with her creative side.

"Oh," Finn and I said at the same time.

"So, what do you need permission for?" she asked.

I gulped, wishing I'd had more time to prepare my defense. "Babysitting," I said, sitting up straighter and speaking with as much confidence as I could muster.

"On Saturday night. Lisa and Caroline want to celebrate their anniversary. And the last time they took Beckett to a restaurant, he poured water on the busboy. The owner asked them not to return, and they're running out of local restaurants they're allowed to show their faces in."

"You went and got yourself another job?" Mom asked. "Are you sure you have time for all this? What about school? And fun?"

"Told you," Finn whispered.

I ignored him, as usual, and turned to my mom. "Dog walking *is* fun, and I still have plenty of time for homework. Please let me try it for one night, and I'll see how it goes. You're the one who wanted us to take that babysitting course; what's the point of all that knowledge if I'm not putting it to work? Plus, hopefully Finn can start babysitting for them, too. It'll be good for him. You know—it'll keep him off the streets." I poked my brother's side.

Finn slapped my hand away. "Yeah, I'm really at risk here."

"You make a well-argued case," Mom said, in her best lawyer tone.

Did I mention my mom is a lawyer?

No?

My mom is a lawyer.

Mom considered my plea for a few moments before answering.

"Okay. You can try it next weekend. Please leave me the address. And didn't Beckett's family just move? Where are they now?"

"They're two blocks away," I told her, "at Eighth Avenue and Carroll Street."

"You mean near the old Adams family mansion?" my mom asked. "Doesn't Beatrix live in that high-rise, too?"

"They're not in the high-rise," I said. "They moved into the mansion. Or at least, they're in one of the apartments. The one on the fifth floor."

"I didn't realize people were still willing to live there," she said. "They must've gotten a really good deal."

"What do you mean?" I asked.

This funny expression came over my mom's face. Her eyes—normally so alert, too perceptive for me and Finn to get away with anything—went vacant.

Oh, and she didn't bother answering my question.

"Mom?" I asked.

She stared off into space as if she'd been fully zombified.

"Hey, Mom?" I repeated, louder this time.

No reply. She was starting to scare me.

"MOM!" I screamed.

She finally snapped out of it. "What?" she asked, blinking at me in confusion, as if she hadn't heard me talking to her for the past few minutes.

"So, can I do it? Babysit, I mean."

"Sure," she said. "If you want to."

"I do," I said. "And why do you seem so surprised? About the mansion, I mean."

"No reason," she said quickly.

"Are you sure?" I asked. "Because I've heard about the rumors about the ghost of Margaret. Don't tell me you believe in ghosts, too."

"What rumors? I'm going to get started on dinner," she said. Which, I don't need to point out, was not exactly the answer I was looking for. Or any answer at all, for that matter. But I decided to let it go, because Sonya was calling.

I picked up my cell and said, "Hey, what's up?"

"You tell me," said Sonya. "Do you have any leads on the ice-cream-parlor sabotage?"

"Ugh, not yet," I said as I wandered into my room and sat down cross-legged on the floor. "Sorry; it's been a hectic afternoon. I'll try to come over to the store tomorrow. Will it be open?"

"Absolutely," said Sonya. "We're not going to be intimidated by anyone. I'm not, anyway. My mom is freaking out, though. She's already talking about shutting down the business."

"Because of one window?" I asked.

"That's exactly what I said," Sonya told me. "But I get why she's freaked. Opening this business was a lot more expensive than she thought it would be. If it's not a success, well . . . I don't know what, exactly. But it's not going to be good."

"I'll swing by first thing and see if I can figure something out."

"That's perfect. Thanks so much," Sonya gushed. "We open at ten."

"I know," I said.

"See? You're so smart. You'll figure everything out in no time."

"No pressure," I said.

"Oh, there's lots of pressure," Sonya assured me.

"I know. I was kidding. Anyway, I'll see you there."

"Thanks, Maggie. You're the best. I knew we could count on you."

I wanted to remind her that I hadn't actually done anything yet, but she hung up before I had the chance. I headed back into the living room and sat down next to Finn. He was watching some reality show.

"What's this?" I asked.

"Don't know," Finn replied.

The show seemed to be about a bunch of grizzled old geezers with long, scraggly beards.

"Is it good?" I asked.

"Nope," said Finn, his eyes glued to the screen.

I pulled out my new spy notebook. Lulu made it for me as a present after solving my last mystery—finding her retainer before her parents discovered it was missing.

(This involved Dumpster diving, which is all I'm gonna say.) Anyway, the notebook says MAGGIE BROOKLYN, DOG-WALKING DETECTIVE across the front in sparkly rainbow colors. Using it makes me feel half cool private investigator and half dorky kid playing a game. Except the mysteries I solve are real, so I don't know why I get self-conscious about it sometimes. Anyway, flipping to a fresh page in my notebook, I made a list.

THE SABOTAGE OF SONYA'S SWEETS

1) Who broke the window? And how?
2) What was their motive?
3) Where are they now?
4) How am I supposed to figure any of this out?

From there I was stumped.

I'm glad Sonya had faith in me, but her confidence put a lot of pressure on me, too. Just because I'd solved a bunch of mysteries in the past didn't mean I could solve every mystery in the world. What if this one left me clueless? It's not like I had a lot of clues to go on. Oh, but there was the note:

The evidence: one threatening note, printed on the back of a box of Thin Mints Girl Scout cookies in blue highlighter. Neat penmanship. Ominous words.

"What are you doing?" Finn asked, turning off the TV.

"Trying to solve the case of the Sabotage of Sonya's Sweets," I said.

Finn laughed. "I like that you've actually named your case. That's oh-so-Nancy-Drew of you!"

I threw a throw pillow at Finn's head. "If you're going to make fun, I won't bother talking to you," I said.

"Sorry, I was only trying to help. You seem so stressed out."

"I'm fine," I said, closing my notebook. The case worried me, but that wasn't all that was on my mind. I'd texted Milo and called him, too, but hadn't heard a word from him since he stormed off earlier today. All the radio silence left me feeling unsettled.

"Dinner's ready," my mom called, peeking into the living room.

"Where's Dad?" Finn asked as we headed to the table.

"He's out with a friend," said Mom. "So it's just us."

"Oh," I said.

"Finn, did you finish your homework?" she asked.

"It's Saturday night," said Finn.

"Yes, and I thought you wanted to go to that movie with Lulu later."

"I do," Finn said. "Which is exactly why I finished

my homework this afternoon. I'll show you as soon as we're done eating."

"That sounds great," Mom said.

"Hey, how come you're not asking Maggie?" Finn wondered.

"Because she already told me she did her homework yesterday," Mom said. "And I saw it."

"Right," I said. "I finished early because I had such a busy day, between the Sonya's Sweets opening and walking Nofarm at his new house at Eighth Avenue and Carroll. In that so-called haunted mansion."

Our mom grabbed some bread out of the bread basket and ripped off a small piece. "So, how would you two feel about going away this Christmas?" she asked. "Dad and I were talking about taking a vacation. Maybe to Costa Rica."

"Can Lulu come?" asked Finn.

Mom glared at him. "No, your girlfriend cannot come on our family vacation."

"But she's Maggie's best friend," Finn tried. "So it's a win-win."

I shook my head. "Dude, you are pathetic!"

"But it's true," said Finn. He continued to make his case, but I wasn't paying attention anymore. I couldn't help but notice that every time I brought up the haunted mansion, my mom changed the subject.

I tried calling Milo after dinner, but his phone kept going straight to voice mail. He must be avoiding my calls.

I never would've laughed at him if I'd known he was that serious about the ghost thing.

Not right to his face, anyway.

"You're not doing anything tonight?" asked Finn, as he changed from one stained sweatshirt into another, less-stained sweatshirt.

"Everyone's busy," I said.

"Want to come out with me and Lulu?" Finn asked.

I huffed out a small breath. "It's weird enough that you're going out with my best friend. I don't need to go out on dates with you all the time, too. I mean, once a day is enough, believe me."

"Sorry for trying to keep you from staying home alone on a Saturday night," said Finn.

"I'm not alone. Mom's around," I said. "Plus, I have a lot to do."

"You already told me you finished your homework," said Finn.

"Don't you need to get ready?" I asked. "Take a shower or something?"

"Why, am I smelly?" Finn asked, sniffing under his arms.

"No more than usual," I replied.

"Oh, you're so funny I forgot to laugh," said Finn. And he headed into our room before I could even respond.

Not that I needed to.

I mean, Finn's response? Way weak, and if that was the best he could do, then I'd clearly won that round.

# Chapter 7

• • •

My mom and I ended up having a lovely evening on the couch watching some old movies: the original *Willy Wonka & the Chocolate Factory* and then *The Sound of Music*, because we both love musicals.

It was nice to be distracted from the fact that Milo was ignoring me, and that I had a big mystery to solve with basically zero leads.

Of course, once I was in bed that night, all the stress and worry came rushing back. I couldn't sleep because my mind kept going back over the day's weirdness. The harsh sound of shattering glass replayed in my head, which just reminded me of the broken mirror at Nofarm's house. Which brought me back to the whole Milo situation.

At some point in the night I must've drifted off to sleep, because hours later I woke up in a cold sweat.

My hair was plastered to my face, and I huffed and puffed like some big bad wolf trying to blow down a house. My heart raced as if I'd been sprinting for miles.

"Are you okay?" asked Finn, who must've heard me from the other side of the room.

"No," I said. "I mean, yeah. I'm fine." I looked around the room. As my eyes adjusted to the darkness, the bedroom furniture came into focus—bookshelf dividing my side of the room from Finn's to my left, desk straight ahead, fireplace facade to the right. It all provided me some comfort.

I took a deep breath in through my nose, filling my chest with air and pausing for a moment before exhaling, something I learned during our yoga unit in gym class. At the moment, though, it did little to calm me down.

"What's wrong?" asked Finn.

"Nothing," I said, not wanting to admit the truth. I'd had a nightmare, but this was no ordinary nightmare. It felt way more scary, more intense and real. I don't even remember all the details—just the sensations.

I was in a dark and scary place, and something was wrapped tightly around my body. It constricted my chest and made it near impossible to breathe. But when I looked down I couldn't see a thing, because nothing was there. And yet that nothing pressed into me, squeezing me from all sides. The air seemed to disappear from the room, and I wondered whether I could drown even though there wasn't any water in sight.

My arms were free, so I tried to claw at this invisible thing, but I couldn't feel it.

Yet still it squeezed tighter and tighter and tighter.

When I tried to run, I couldn't make my legs work.

All I could do was sit in the small room with the dark walls closing in around me, creepy organ music blasting in my ears.

I couldn't even call for help, because my voice didn't work.

Even though I was awake now, with plenty of oxygen in my fairly large bedroom, I was still trembling.

"Sorry," I said to Finn. "Did you hear me tossing and turning?"

"No, I heard you screaming."

"What do you mean?" I asked.

I heard the rustle of sheets and the creak of the bed as Finn sat up. "You were screaming your own name."

I sat up myself, because this didn't make any sense. I didn't recall using my voice.

"Seriously?" I asked. "I was screaming 'Maggie'?"

"Not Maggie," said Finn. "You were screaming your real name: Margaret."

# Chapter 8

◆ ◆ ◆

I showed up at Sonya's Sweets at a quarter to ten to find the picture window covered with two large pieces of crisscrossed plywood. Someone had scrawled "OPEN" on one of them in all capital letters with a red Sharpie. It was functional, but a far cry from yesterday's gorgeous welcome sign.

When I knocked on the front door, Sonya's cousin, Felicity, looked up from the countertop she was cleaning at the back of the store. She seemed surprised to see me. "We're closed," she called.

At least, I think she said that. My lip-reading skills are decent but not perfect.

"I know," I said, nodding and pointing to the door. "Can you let me in anyway?"

She walked over to Joshua, who was mopping up behind the counter. They talked, then he looked at me and nodded and gave me the thumbs-up sign. Felicity walked over and opened the door a crack.

"We met yesterday, remember? I'm Sonya's friend, Maggie."

Felicity opened up the door a bit more so I could squeeze through. "Right. Ricki mentioned you might stop by. Please excuse the mess."

"Don't worry about it," I replied as I looked around the store. "Okay if we sit down for a minute and talk?"

She looked around nervously. "Um, I have a lot to do before we open. This isn't the best—"

"This will only take a few minutes," I said, interrupting. "Ten at the most, and then I'll leave you alone."

"It's okay, Felicity," Joshua called from across the store. "I'll cover for you."

Felicity didn't say anything, but I could tell by the look on her face that she wasn't thrilled with his offer.

I walked over to the nearest booth and took a seat before she could change her mind. "Please join me," I said, whipping out my notebook and looking up at her expectantly.

Felicity sank down into the booth across from me. She was pretty, like Sonya, and they were both tall and thin and long-limbed.

Of course, Sonya is tall for a seventh grader, and Felicity is just plain tall for anyone. Except for maybe a basketball player. Then she'd be average. Or perhaps below average, but only a bit. I think. I actually don't know the average height of professional basketball players. I could look it up; I suppose that's what Wikipedia is for. Or there's math, if the statistic isn't readily available. But who has time for that? Not me—I had interviews to conduct.

"So, how long have you been in Brooklyn?" I asked.

"Just a few weeks," said Felicity.

"Sonya told me you're from Indiana?"

Felicity nodded.

"Indiana's pretty far from here, huh?" I said.

Felicity rolled her eyes. "Tell me about it. I'm from the tiniest town in the middle of nowhere. It's the exact opposite of New York. This is the first real city I've ever been to, unless you count Chicago. I was there once on a school trip." She fiddled with the salt and pepper shakers as she spoke, staring at them rather than meeting my eye.

I couldn't help but notice that as Felicity talked, she kind of rambled on. I wondered whether that was always the case or she was nervous about speaking with me in particular. And if so, why? Did she have a legitimate reason to be worried?

Just then Joshua came over with two mugs of hot chocolate. "Here you go," he said. "These are on the house."

"Thanks," I said. "But what are they for?"

Joshua shrugged. "I don't know. You looked thirsty."

I took a sip. "Mmm. That's delicious!"

"Joshua makes the best hot chocolate," Felicity said, smiling up at him.

"Old family recipe," Joshua said with a wink.

Felicity turned back to me. "Did you have any more questions, or can I get back to work now?"

"I'm actually just getting started," I said, checking my notes again. "Um, what brought you to New York, exactly?"

"You're writing all of this down?" she asked, glancing at my notebook.

"I remember things better when I write them down. And sometimes it helps me make connections later."

Felicity swirled her spoon around in her mug, and some cocoa splashed over the edge. "Oh no!" she cried, alarmed. And when she reached for the napkins to clean up the hot chocolate, she knocked over the entire mug with the back of her hand. Hot chocolate spilled all over the table, and the mug began to roll.

Felicity reached for it, but rather than standing it upright she pushed it off the edge and it shattered on the floor.

"Yikes!" she yelled.

I cringed.

Joshua ran over with the mop to clean up the mess.

I had to wonder, was Felicity nervous, or simply klutzy? Or was she pretending to be klutzy because she was bent on sabotage? Or was I jumping to conclusions too fast? Why would she want to ruin her aunt's new shop—her aunt who was responsible for Felicity having a place to stay in New York City?

I drew a big question mark in my notebook. I would've written down more specific questions, except Felicity was squinting down at the page as if she were trying to read my notes upside down. I wondered why she was so interested. Her behavior made me even more suspicious.

"What are you," she asked, "some sort of junior police officer?"

"Um, I'm more of an amateur detective," I said, watching her carefully. She didn't seem to be making fun of me, but the question seemed odd.

"You mean like Nancy Drew?" she asked. "I used to read those books all the time."

"Kind of," I said. "So, how are you related to Sonya, exactly?"

"We're first cousins. Our moms are sisters."

"How old are you?"

"Eighteen," she said. "I was supposed to start college this year, but I'm taking a gap year instead."

"So you work at the Gap, too?" I asked.

"No." Felicity laughed. "A gap year means a year off. I'm supposed to be finding myself, figuring out who I am and what I want to do with my life. That way, college won't be a waste of time. My parents don't think I have enough direction, so they sent me here to Brooklyn."

"Do you agree with them?" I asked.

"No. I've got plenty of direction—I just don't want to move in the direction they want me to. Here's the real story: I want to go to art school and my parents want me to go to business school. We couldn't agree, so as a compromise I'm taking time to explore both art and business."

"That makes sense," I said.

"In theory, yes," said Felicity. "I'm taking a figure-painting class at Pratt, the art college in Brooklyn. Working here was part of the deal, because it's giving me experience with business. Plus, I need the money, because my parents want to teach me the value of a dollar. Whatever that means!"

"So how do you feel about working at Sonya's Sweets?" I asked. "It sounds like you're not so excited about it."

"It's fine," she said with a shrug. "You know—except for all of the flying glass. I guess you could say it's a lot more exciting than I thought it would be." She peeked over her shoulder toward Joshua.

"Let's talk about the flying glass," I said. "Do you have any idea who would have destroyed such a gorgeous window?"

"Not a clue," Sonya replied quickly. "That's what we're all wondering—right?"

"Did you notice anything suspicious yesterday? Or any customers who seemed particularly odd?"

"I was too busy working," said Sonya. "Check out my hands. They're totally wrinkled from all the dishes I've had to wash."

Sonya held out her hands, palms facing me. They did look a bit prune-y. Her nails had specks of green and blue around the edges. She noticed me noticing them.

"That's paint, but it won't come off no matter what," said Sonya.

"What are you working on?" I asked.

"We're doing self-portraits," said Sonya. "Which aren't my favorite thing, but my teacher is amazing."

"Sonya told me you're living with her family," I said.

"Yup. Sonya and I share a room and everything. It's like we're suddenly sisters, which is funny because we're both only children."

Felicity looked behind her again. Joshua, I noticed, was lingering in the background. He kept mopping the same two feet of floor, the tiles of which were already sparkling. He was obviously eavesdropping. I didn't mind, exactly; I just found it strange.

I put the letter *J* for "Joshua" in my notebook. Sonya pretended not to read it, but I saw her eyes narrow into a squint.

I turned to a fresh page and said, "Sonya and her mom are pretty excited about the soda fountain."

"I know," said Felicity. "It's all they've been talking about since I've been here."

"They've got a lot riding on it," I said. "So let me ask you again—do you have any idea who might have broken the window?"

Felicity shook her head. "Nope."

I wasn't getting very far, which frustrated me. On some level I knew what the problem was. Detectives aren't supposed to ask yes or no questions. Leading questions—the kind that require more thought and explanation—are how you get interesting information. So, for example, I shouldn't have asked Felicity where she was from. I should've said, "Tell me about yourself."

But for some reason—maybe it was the fact that Felicity was already so uncomfortable—things just didn't pan out that way.

Joshua was outside now, sweeping the sidewalk. I lowered my voice and pointed to him. "How well do you know that guy?"

"Who?" Felicity asked, even though there wasn't anyone else in front of the shop.

"Joshua," I said. "That's his name, right?"

"Oh, him? I guess that's his name. I can't really keep track." She brushed her bangs off her face and rolled her eyes. "I'm so bad with names. In fact, I'm bad with faces, too."

"But he just brought us hot chocolate. And he's the only other employee here. The only one you're not related to, that is." I couldn't believe I had to point this out.

Felicity turned bright red. "That's true. I guess I do know who you're talking about, but I hardly know him. I swear."

Felicity was a bad liar. Not only did she completely fumble her answer, but I had hard evidence proving the opposite of what she was saying. Yesterday at the opening she and Joshua were totally chummy. They spent the whole afternoon joking around and talking; even after the glass shattered they'd been laughing about something.

So why was she pretending she didn't know who he was now? It made no sense, unless she was hiding her relationship with him for some other reason. My mind raced as I tried to make the connections.

Maybe Joshua was responsible for the picture-window destruction but Felicity didn't realize it until today, which was why she was trying to distance herself from him now.

Or maybe Felicity was responsible and she was

trying to frame Joshua somehow. Unless they were working together . . . But if it was just the two of them, how did they manage to break the window from the outside? And what could be their motive?

"Did you hear about the salty pie?" I asked Felicity. "I'm wondering if maybe there's a connection. Like, maybe the person who destroyed the window was working from inside the shop."

I noticed that Felicity was suddenly alert and staring straight at me. She had this funny expression on her face—a type of frozen fear, like a deer caught in the headlights.

Maybe I was finally getting somewhere. I waited, watching.

"There's no connection, I swear," she said.

"How can you be so sure?" I asked.

"Because I did it," Felicity blurted out, covering her face in her hands. "I mixed up the salt and sugar. I'm so sorry. It was ridiculous. It wasn't just the pie you had that was ruined—I destroyed all ten of them. I feel so bad for my aunt Ricki, and I should've told her the truth yesterday but I was too embarrassed."

"I see," I said, writing this down.

"Are you going to tell Aunt Ricki?" Felicity asked.

"Um, I don't know," I said. "Do you think I shouldn't?"

"I'm just too embarrassed about it," said Felicity.

She leaned in closer and whispered. “Do me a favor? Don’t say anything, and I’ll tell her in my own time.”

“I don’t want to be a tattletale,” I said. “So I guess if it doesn’t come up, I won’t mention it. But if she asks me . . .”

“Sure, sure, sure,” said Felicity. “That totally makes sense. If she asks you, fine. But why would she? I’ll tell her eventually, I promise. Thanks, Maggie. You’re the best.” She jumped up and gave me a hug that smelled of vanilla perfume. “Okay, I’ve really gotta run. We’re supposed to open soon, and my aunt will be here any minute. She’s not going to be happy if things aren’t set up exactly the way she wants them.”

Felicity was gone before I could ask her another question. I flipped through my notes, searching for any useful information, but couldn’t find any. Based on what I knew, it was not surprising that Felicity had mixed up the salt and sugar.

But was she really just klutzy and awkward? Or was she hiding something?

# Chapter 9

◆ ◆ ◆

Just then, a customer walked in through the door. Three customers, actually. Well, two adults pushing a red stroller with a dark-haired baby inside. "Are you open yet?" asked the mom.

"Not yet," said Felicity. "Why don't you come back at noon?"

"Hey, wait!" Joshua called from behind the counter. "We open at ten o'clock, and it's already five minutes past."

"Oops, sorry about that," said Felicity. She walked up to the customers and said, "Please take a menu. I'll get you some seats."

The couple stood there, confused.

"She means please take a seat and she'll get you some menus," Joshua explained.

Felicity ran her fingers through her loose dark hair.

It was supposed to be up in a ponytail, a bun, or a braid, and her paper soda-jerk hat was missing, too. "Isn't that what I said?" she asked.

"Almost," said Joshua with a sweet smile. "You sure you've got this covered?"

"Of course," said Felicity. "You keep doing, whatever it was you were doing."

"Hey, you're Joshua, right?" I asked, hopping onto a barstool.

"Guilty as charged," said Joshua, smiling to reveal perfectly straight, white teeth. "You're Sonya's friend?"

"Maggie Brooklyn," I said, holding out my hand.

Joshua shook it. His fingernails were painted black, and he had a tattoo of a miniature chocolate bar on his wrist. A chocolate bar? I wanted to ask. Why? But I didn't mention it, because I had more important questions for him. Plus, I figured no explanation would really suffice.

"So, Sonya and her mom asked me to look into the whole picture-window breakage thing," I explained.

"I know," said Joshua.

"Right," I said. "You must've overheard."

He didn't deny this. He just stared straight at me, expectant, like he knew the drill. I found it somewhat unnerving.

"How did you get the job here?" I asked.

"I've known Sonya's family forever," said Joshua.

"My family lives across the street. And I just started college in September and needed a part-time job, so this was perfect. I have experience, too: I used to work at Cupcake Cupcake Cupcake in the city."

"Cupcake Cupcake?" I asked.

"Cupcake," said Joshua. "There are three of them. Were, anyway. It was a small bakery in the city. Used to be really popular, but it closed down last year."

"How come?" I asked.

Joshua shrugged. "I don't know. Cupcakes aren't as popular as they used to be, I guess. That's why Ricki is so smart. This place serves all sorts of desserts, and it's got a theme: old-fashioned soda fountain. She really put a lot of thought into it, and tons of work, too. It's a shame, what's been going on."

"Any theories as to who might've broken the window?" I asked.

"Nope," said Joshua. "I was caught completely off guard. I really don't know who could be behind this sort of thing."

"Did you notice anything strange at the opening?" I asked.

"Strange, how?" he asked. "The place was packed, and I was busy cleaning up, pouring water, and selling cupcakes and cookies and pie."

"Ugh, don't remind me of pie," I said, clutching my stomach. "Just hearing the word makes me want to gag."

"Oh, was that you who ended up with the salty bite?" asked Joshua.

"It sure was," I said.

"Sorry about that," he said.

"Oh, don't worry about it." I was about to tell him that Felicity already explained the mix-up, but then something occurred to me. "Wait. Why are you apologizing?"

"Because it was my fault," said Joshua. "Stupid mistake. Everything got so hectic on Saturday; I guess I somehow switched the salt and sugar."

"Huh," I said. "I didn't realize."

I wrote this down in my notebook—extra small so he couldn't see. But Joshua wasn't concerned with reading upside down, like Felicity had been; he was still working behind the counter as we spoke, pouring M&M'S into an empty glass jar, refilling napkin holders, changing out the old tub of vanilla ice cream for one that was brand-new.

"Well, that's one mystery solved," said Joshua. "I'm going to confess to Ricki this afternoon. I should've told her yesterday, but everything got too crazy."

Joshua smiled at me again, and a single word popped into my head, seemingly out of nowhere: dazzling. That's when I realized something—Sonya was right. For an old guy with a ponytail and weird tattoos, Joshua was cute, which I found distracting. His eyes were green and vibrant and shaped like sideways apostrophes. They crinkled in the corners in the cutest way when he smiled.

I wanted to look away when he stared straight at me, but I couldn't.

"I am sincerely sorry that I ruined strawberry rhubarb pie for you. Please let me make it up to you," he said, a sly grin tugging at his lips.

"How would you do that?" I asked.

"By giving you this amazing cookie. It's peanut-butter-chocolate-chip—an old family recipe. I used to make them at Cupcake Cupcake Cupcake, and it was the bestselling cookie."

"So the cupcake place sold cookies, too?" I asked.

"They did, but no one knew about it. That was their big problem. One of their problems, anyway."

I took a bite of the cookie, which was still warm from the oven. The entire thing was melty, sweet, salty, and savory—the perfect combination of flavors.

"You baked this?" I asked.

"Yup. I'm a big baker. I want to open up my own place someday. That's why I'm working here—so I can learn all the tricks of the trade." Joshua laughed and winked at me again.

Guys don't wink at me very often, and I'm glad

about that, because when it does happen I never know how I'm supposed to react.

I mean, think about it: someone waves, you wave back.

Someone says hi, you say hi back.

But a wink? You don't wink back. So what do you do?

Seriously—what do you do with a wink?

At the moment, I smiled and blushed and fumbled, completely flummoxed. Then I slid off the stool and said, "Thanks. See you later."

I left the store quickly and headed over to Prospect Park. I had some thinking to do, and the park is my favorite place to wander around and puzzle things out. I headed in through the Third Street entrance and waved to the black stone panthers that flanked the path.

They didn't wave back, but do I even need to point that out?

I walked counterclockwise toward Grand Army Plaza, where the Sunday farmers' market was in full swing.

Strolling along among the apple-cider-doughnut vendors and kale farmers and pickle makers, and a bunch of people stocking up on organic vegetables, I tried to make sense of what I'd just discovered.

Joshua and Felicity had both claimed responsibility

for the salty pie, but clearly only one of them could have done it. So why did they both tell me they were guilty? Who was lying, and what were they covering up?

If I had to guess—and I did, since there wasn't enough evidence to come to any definitive conclusions—something told me Joshua didn't make the mistake. He told me he's an experienced baker, and he kept talking about family recipes. Witnessing his ease and speed behind the counter made me believe him. He knew what he was doing.

Plus, baking requires a precise mind. It's all about chemistry, and measuring things out to the milligram and paying attention to quantity, time, and temperature. Joshua seemed to care about all of those things. He wanted to open up his own dessert place someday, and he even had a chocolate bar tattooed on his wrist. That's passion.

The more I thought about it, the more convinced I was that Joshua didn't make the switch. Not accidentally, anyway. So why did he say he had? What reason could he have for lying to my face?

I wrote his name down in my notebook.

Joshua Marcus.
He may not be guilty of mixing up the salt and sugar.
But he sure is guilty of something.

# Chapter 10

• • •

"Where's Milo?" Lulu asked me at lunch on Tuesday.

"No idea," I said, frowning into my turkey wrap. "He's not in school today."

"Again?" Sonya asked, a worried look on her face. "Is he sick?"

I sighed. "Knowing that would require me actually speaking to Milo. And to speak to Milo, he'd have to call me back. Or respond to my texts. Or send a smoke signal, or tap something out in Morse code, none of which he's actually done."

"You know Morse code?" asked Lulu.

"I'm kidding," I said.

"You think he's still mad about you making fun of him?" asked Beatrix.

"I didn't make fun of him," I said.

"You told us you basically laughed in his face for

believing in ghosts," Lulu reminded me as she twirled a gigantic bundle of spaghetti around her spork.

I cringed. "Okay, I guess I did make fun of him a teensy tiny bit. But I was half joking, and I apologized twice, once via voice mail and once in a text."

"Maybe you should apologize in person," said Beatrix.

"I would love to!" I cried. "But that would require me actually seeing him."

"It's weird that you haven't heard from him in so long," said Beatrix. "He must be really sick."

"How sick does he have to be to not call me back?" I asked.

"Maybe he lost his voice," said Lulu.

"Then why hasn't he texted? I'm sure his fingers still work."

"Maybe we should change the subject," said Lulu, realizing how upset I was.

"How's the investigation going?" asked Sonya. "I hope you come up with something soon, because my mom keeps talking about closing the store."

"But it just opened," I said.

"I know," Sonya said. "But everything is going wrong. Turns out an undercover reporter also tasted the salty pie, and he gave it a lousy review in the *Park Slope Weekly*."

"That's terrible," I said.

"He even took a picture of the shattered window." Sonya pulled the article out of her backpack and smoothed out the newspaper on the table.

The headline read SONYA'S SWEETS IN A STICKY SITUATION.

Lulu groaned. "That can't be good for business," she said.

The photo made me think of something, though. Ricki had a camera around her neck last weekend. "Hey, wasn't your mom taking pictures of opening day?" I asked.

"She was," said Sonya. "And I think Joshua had the camera for a while, too."

"I'd love to see them," I said. "I'm out of leads at the moment, but I'm thinking maybe I'll find something."

"That's a great idea," said Sonya, smiling for the first time all day. "I don't think my mom has downloaded them from the camera yet, but I'll tell her to hurry up with that."

"Good."

"I really hope you figure something out soon. Felicity is driving me crazy! It's bad enough being roomies with her now, but if she's just living with us and not working at the store, she'll be around twenty-four-seven."

"What's wrong with having her around the house?" I asked.

"She's a bathroom hog. And she always wants to watch dumb TV shows. And she keeps me up at night, texting at crazy hours."

"Who is she texting?" I asked.

"Don't know; she's totally super secretive about it," said Sonya. "I looked at her phone, and it's someone she calls 'JAM.' "

" 'JAM'?" I asked.

"Yeah. I think it's her boyfriend, but she won't admit it. Maybe because he's got such a dumb nickname," said Sonya. "When I get older and Joshua and I can be together, I'll only call him by his real name."

I looked at Lulu and Beatrix just to make sure I heard her right. They were both looking at Sonya like she was crazy. So, yeah, I guess I had. But she didn't even notice the weird looks.

"Did you know he told me he'd teach me how to make chocolate cream pie?" Sonya went on. "Can you think of anything more romantic than that?"

" 'Chocolate cream pie' and 'romantic' have probably never been used in the same sentence before," Beatrix said.

"Whatever! Make fun of me now—but guess who's going to be laughing at my and Joshua's wedding in fifteen years?" asked Sonya.

I looked from Beatrix to Lulu to Sonya, and the four of us cracked up.

"Okay, fine," said Sonya. "Maybe I'm getting ahead of myself. But he is super cute and an awesome baker. Speaking of—I brought treats for everyone." She doled out lemon bars to us all.

"Mmm," I said, biting into one. "This is amazing. I love the sweet and sour combination."

"Delicious," said Lulu, polishing off hers in three quick bites and licking her fingers afterward.

Sonya looked to Beatrix, who hadn't even picked her bar up. She stared at it pensively. "Aren't you going to try it, B?" Sonya asked.

"I'm still full from lunch," said Beatrix, placing her palm on her belly. "I'll try it after school, though. It'll be the perfect after-school snack."

"Okay," said Sonya. "But definitely tell me what you think."

"I will," said Beatrix. She looked at her watch and stood up. "I've gotta run. See you guys later?"

"Sure," I said with a wave.

Once she was gone, Sonya said, "We still have ten minutes until the first bell rings. What's up with her?"

Lulu shrugged. "Maybe she's on a diet."

"That would be crazy, because she's super skinny," said Sonya.

I agreed with my friends, but I had bigger things to worry about—like school. "I *so* do not want to go to history right now," I said as I packed up my lunch. "Mr. Phelps is going to have sandwich crumbs stuck in his beard; he always does. Plus, I didn't study for last week's test."

"I'm sure you did fine," said Lulu.

Twenty minutes later I proved Lulu wrong. I held up my test so she could see the big, fat D+ at the top of the page.

"Sorry," she whispered.

I shrugged. Worse than my lousy grade was the note from Mr. Phelps: *Please see me after class.*

History ran longer than usual, and when the bell finally rang I dragged myself slowly to the front of the room. I couldn't help but feel totally queasy, because the thing is, I usually do pretty well in school. I'm not a straight-A student or anything, but I'd never gotten a D+ before.

"Sorry about the test," I said.

"I am, too," said Mr. Phelps, crossing his arms over his chest. When he frowned, the crumbs in his beard moved but didn't fall out. "What happened?"

I shrugged. "I don't know. I guess I didn't study enough."

"Did you study at all?" he asked.

I didn't know how to answer him because I couldn't admit that his class bored me to tears, or that every time I tried to open the textbook I got sleepy. "It won't happen again," I promised.

"I hope not. You're normally a better student, Maggie. Everyone can have bad luck on a test; I don't want this to ruin your grade for the entire semester. That's why I'm going to give you the opportunity to earn some extra credit. You can write a report. If it's good, and thorough, then I'll bring your grade up a letter."

"To a C-plus?" I asked.

"Yes—which is not amazing because I know you can do better. But it's a start, at least."

"Thanks, Mr. Phelps." I blinked and nodded. "I'll take it. And I need it, too. I've never gotten a D before."

"D-plus," Mr. Phelps said.

"Not much better," I said. "Um, what's the assignment?"

Mr. Phelps ran one hand down his beard, which only served to lodge the crumbs more firmly in place.

"Pick a famous person in history and write about his or her life," he said.

"I can choose anyone?" I asked.

"Anyone from the past, yes," said Mr. Phelps.

"Does the person have to be famous?" I asked. "Because I'd like to write about a maid who immigrated here from Ireland a hundred years ago. She worked for

Jonas Adams—you know, the guy who built the chocolate factory here in Park Slope. So she's not famous, exactly; but she worked for someone who was. Famous, that is."

Mr. Phelps smiled. "So you're telling me you want to write about the ghost who lives in Jonas Adams's house?"

"You know about the haunted mansion?" I asked, surprised. "I mean, the mansion that's rumored to be haunted."

"I've lived in this town for thirty years, and every so often the ghost of Margaret makes an appearance and rumors circulate," he explained. "And I agree with you—writing about her life sounds like a fine project, but you might have a hard time finding much information on Margaret. Why don't you write about Irish immigrants in general? And you can definitely research Margaret's real story and include anything you find. Maybe you'll want to read about Jonas Adams, too. You know, for context. I'm sure you'll learn a lot."

"Okay," I said with a nod. "That sounds great."

"I agree. I'd like three typed pages within the next three weeks."

"That's no problem, Mr. Phelps."

"Oh, and one more thing: I'll need you to have your parents sign the test."

I cringed at this news. "Are you sure that's necessary?" I asked. "I promise to do better. Seriously—this will never happen again. You said yourself that I'm normally a better student."

"I believe you, but I still need the signatures," said Mr. Phelps.

"My mom is going to flip out," I said. "My entire social life will be over. And she'll make me quit my job."

"You have a job?"

"I walk dogs after school," I said. "And I love it. And these dogs depend on me. I can't give it up. Do I really have to get my parents to sign the test? I promise this will never happen again. I'll even write a five-page paper if you want."

"I'm sorry, Maggie, but this is school policy. Any students who get a grade under a C-minus must inform their parents or guardians." Mr. Phelps thought for a moment. "The only thing I can do is give you more time. How about this—get me the signed test by next week, when you turn in the extra-credit assignment."

"Okay," I said. "I'll do that. Thank you. I really appreciate it."

"Good," said Mr. Phelps. "Now please get to your next class, and try not to get anymore Ds this year."

"I won't. I mean, I'll try not to," I said. "See you later."

. . .

The rest of the day passed in a blur, and I could hardly focus on my classes. My mind felt totally cluttered because of everything going on in my life: a lousy test for my parents to sign, a boyfriend who won't speak to me, and a mystery I can't solve. I couldn't see things getting any worse.

As soon as school ended I raced off campus, hoping to find comfort in my regular routine. I was still a dog walker, for this week anyway. And I wasn't ready to turn in my leashes.

My first stop was Bean, the six-pound Maltese. She's my best-dressed dog with the worst attitude. Basically, she snarls, barks, or yaps at anything with a pulse. Today was no exception: her cotton blouse was black with purple stripes on it, her matching cap fell off when she lunged for a squirrel that was almost the same size as her, and she almost tripped on her tie when she tried to go after a pigeon.

Most days I'm amused by her antics, but today I had no patience. "Come on, Bean," I called as I pulled her in the other direction and retrieved her hat. "Let's skip the park today, okay?"

Bean didn't respond, because she was too busy growling at the bulldog across the street.

"Let's go to Sonya's Sweets," I said. "You'll like it there because you'll be the only dog. Okay, sweetie pie?

And as you know, I'm only calling you 'sweetie pie' ironically."

I scooped up Bean and carried her the rest of the way.

When I got to Sonya's Sweets, I found both Sonya and Ricki busy behind the counter. The place was packed.

"Is it okay if I come in with her?" I asked, pointing to Bean.

"Of course," said Ricki. "As long as you hold her the whole time. Those are the health department laws, and we all know I can't afford a fine."

"Okay, I'll be careful with her," I said. "Where's Felicity?"

"Great question," said Sonya as she served up a delicious-looking banana split to a young woman in a purple sweaterdress. "She was supposed to be here an hour ago."

"Did you try her cell again?" asked Ricki.

"I did," said Sonya. "And there's still no answer."

"I hope she's okay," said Ricki.

"I'm sure she's fine. All she's got is an acute case of not-wanting-to-go-to-work-itis," said Sonya.

"Leave your cousin alone," said Ricki.

"Why?" asked Sonya. "I have every right to be annoyed. We've been totally swamped because Joshua isn't here either, but at least he called in sick."

"Excuse me, miss?" asked a new customer, an older man wearing a Brookyln Dodgers cap, who stood at the counter.

"I'm on it," said Sonya, heading over to where he stood. "Can I help you, sir?"

"I'll take two dozen chocolate-chip cookies to go," he said.

"Oh, we don't have any cookies at the moment because we're all out of chocolate chips," said Sonya.

"What do you mean, you're out of chocolate chips?"

"The shipment never came in," said Sonya, forcing a smile. "Or it got lost. We're not sure, because we're still trying to track it down. Why don't you try the apple pie instead? It's delicious."

"I had my heart set on something chocolaty," said the man.

"We're hoping it comes in later; perhaps you could try back tonight?" asked Sonya.

"Or maybe I could just go to the Cocoa Bar down the street," he said, handing back the menu and heading outside.

"Well, that's an option, too," Sonya whispered to herself. "If you want to be a jerk about it."

"What's that about?" I asked.

"Don't ask," said Sonya. "Oh, wait—you already did, so I'll tell you. None of our supplies arrived this morning, so we couldn't bake anything fresh." She glanced at her mom, who was on the phone, seemingly stressed out. "My mom is talking with the supplier now.

A few seconds later, Ricki hung up and walked over to us. "They claimed they delivered everything this morning and someone named Samoa signed for it, Ricki said."

"Samoa?" asked Sonya. "I've never heard of that name before."

I pulled out my notebook and wrote this down.

Missing chocolate—signed for by Samoa.

Then I stared at my note, hoping it would spark an idea. But no— I had nothing else to write, so I put the notebook away.

Meanwhile, Ricki paced back and forth across the shop, looking super stressed. She pressed her fingers to her temples. "I have the worst headache. Who told me running a soda fountain would be fun and profitable? This job is stressful, and it's costing us a fortune!"

"It's going to be okay," said Sonya.

"Maybe it's time to close up shop," said Ricki. "I mean, at this rate, why delay the inevitable?"

"We can't close the store because of one tiny little missing box of chocolate," said Sonya.

"It's actually a very large box, and as you know, we have a gazillion other little problems."

"Come on, Mom. We're fine. This is business as usual. It's—"

But before Sonya finished her thought, the lights went out.

# Chapter 11

• • •

Things go wrong when you open a new business. That's what Ricki assured her customers as she escorted them out the door with a smile.

"Come back soon," she called. "I'm sure the power will be on in no time."

"Yeah, right," said Sonya once everyone was gone.

"Hush, someone will hear you," said Ricki as she flipped the sign from OPEN to CLOSED and locked the doors from the inside. "There's got to be an explanation for this. I'm going to go out back and check the wires."

"Sorry about this," I said as I shifted Bean from one arm to the other.

Sonya reached out to pet Bean but the dog bared her teeth, so she pulled her hand away.

"Has your mom uploaded the pictures from the opening yet?" I asked.

"Nope." Sonya shook her head. "With everything

going on, she hasn't had a moment of free time. Plus, I think she lost the cable. I'm sure it'll turn up, though. Or maybe not. Maybe that'll be one more problem we have."

"I'm sorry, Sonya." I didn't know what else to say.

We sat in the dark for a few moments until Sonya broke the silence. "My dad is worried about us. He's even thinking about coming home from India, which would be bad, because he's in the middle of a really big deal there."

Before I could say anything, Ricki came back inside. "The circuit breakers look good," she said.

"Then why is the power off?" Sonya asked. "Did you forget to pay the bill or something?"

"I paid the bill. Felicity mailed the check for me."

"Ha!" Sonya said. "Are you sure about that?"

"She was supposed to," said Ricki, suddenly sounding a bit worried. "Let me try calling her again."

But as Ricki pulled her phone from her back pocket, Felicity appeared at the door. She tried to push it open but it was locked, so she rattled the door and knocked on the glass.

Sonya ran over to let her in.

"Why are we closed?" asked Felicity. "I wish I'd known so I wouldn't have had to come." She glanced at me and Bean. "Hi, there. Cute doggie."

Bean growled at her.

"I cannot believe you said that when you stroll in here two hours late." Then Sonya practically growled at Felicity.

Felicity looked at her watch. "What do you mean? It's three o'clock."

"It's almost five," said Sonya.

Felicity didn't answer because she was squinting down at the face of her watch. "I guess my watch stopped," she said.

"And two hours passed without you even noticing?" asked Sonya. "How can anyone be that spacey?"

"Sonya, don't scold your cousin. She's my employee, not yours," Ricki said.

"Sorry I'm late, Aunt Ricki," said Felicity. "It was an innocent mistake. We were at the Museum of Modern Art and I lost track of time. It always happens when I go."

"Who's 'we'?" I asked.

Felicity turned around to look at me, blinking with surprise. "What do you mean?"

"You said 'we were at the museum.' "

"No, I didn't. I said *I* was there. At least, that's what I meant. Who would I go to the museum with? I don't know anyone in New York." Eyes wide, Felicity raised her shoulders in an exaggerated shrug.

"Come on," said Sonya. "Why don't you admit it? You were with JAM."

"Who?" asked Felicity, still playing dumb.

"Stop denying it!" Sonya said. "I know you have some super-secret boyfriend or whatever. So who is he?"

Ricki stepped between Felicity and Sonya. "Please stop fighting, girls. We've got bigger problems. The power is out because the bill never got paid. Felicity, dear, I gave you that envelope to mail two weeks ago, remember?"

"Of course I do," said Felicity, nodding her head.

"And did you mail it?"

"Totally! I put it in my purse and walked to the post office to buy stamps, and stopped at Kiwi to buy a sweater because it was cold and the sweater in the window was really cute, and then I went to the newsstand to see if they had the new issue of *Vogue*, and then I . . ." Felicity's voice trailed off. She stopped in the middle of braiding her hair.

"And then you forgot to go to the post office?" Sonya asked.

"No. I went to the post office," said Felicity. "But the line was too long, so I left and decided to go back later."

"And when did you go back?" asked Ricki.

"Um, I'm still meaning to," said Felicity. She reached into her gigantic red patent-leather purse, dug around, and pulled out a wrinkled envelope. "See, I have the envelope right here. I'm totally going to mail it. In fact, I'll go to the post office right this second. Hold on."

"Don't go anywhere!" said Ricki. She took the envelope out of Felicity's hands and ripped it up. "I'll call and pay the bill with my credit card. That way they'll get the lights on faster."

"Good thinking. You're so smart," said Felicity.

Ricki sighed. "I should've done that in the first place. But at least we know no one cut the power lines to the building."

"I still think someone has it out for us," said Sonya, glaring at her cousin. "I just didn't realize I'd be related to that person."

When Ricki looked away, Felicitiy stuck her tongue out at Sonya.

I tried not to laugh. The two of them were acting like me and Finn. Or, more accurately, they were fighting like Finn and I used to when we were about five years old.

"We'll be fine," said Ricki. "I'll just pull back all the curtains and put candles out on the tables. It'll be romantic."

"Great," said Felicity. "Problem solved." Then she sat down at one of the tables, pulled out her cell phone, and started to text.

I left the shop quickly, brought Bean back home,

and then walked the rest of my dogs. After that I went home and took some more notes.

Did Felicity forget to pay the electric bill? Or did she hold on to it on purpose? Did her watch really stop, or was she just making an excuse? And whom did she go to the museum with? Was it JAM, the person she's been texting? If so, who is JAM? And why is she keeping his identity a secret?

I spent the rest of the evening trying to answer those questions, but didn't come to any conclusions.

# Chapter 12

◆ ◆ ◆

When Saturday night rolled around, I showed up early to Beckett's house—and I showed up prepared. I lugged my biggest tote bag, filled with a bunch of fun stuff. Or at least, stuff I thought would be fun for a three-year-old: washable Magic Markers, the leftover clay from my Claymation workshop, scissors, and plenty of paper in all different colors. I'd also studied up on knock-knock jokes. Hopefully he wouldn't think they were all dumb.

I was a little nervous, but not about any potential ghosts. *Rumors* of ghosts, I mean. I don't believe in ghosts. I was nervous about humans. Well, one human in particular: Beckett. Taking care of dogs is one thing; I've been doing it for a while, and I know the score. But taking care of an actual human being? A three-year-old boy with a huge capacity for mischief and mayhem? That was going to be hard.

Of course, that's not all that worried me. In the back of my mind I also feared that Beckett didn't like me. We'd never spent much time together, and usually when I picked up Nofarm, Beckett completely ignored me.

The kid is only three years old, but I had jitters similar to the ones I felt before Milo and I went out on a date. Back when Milo and I actually went out on dates, that is. He hadn't been at school all week, and I still hadn't heard from him. I didn't know whether I should feel nervous for him or angry with him. At the moment, I felt both.

Also? I couldn't help but think at least a little bit about the ghost of Margaret. Like I said, I don't believe in ghosts, but the story of her demise gave me the creepy crawlies.

When I knocked on the door, someone shouted, "Door's open," so I walked inside.

Beckett sat on the living-room floor, playing with blocks. He wore space-themed pajamas, dark blue with starbursts and rocket ships shooting across the front. When he saw me, he raced over and butted his head into my stomach.

"Yeeouch!" I shouted. Because being sucker punched—sorry, sucker headed—in the stomach? It hurts.

And let me tell you, Beckett's ample mound of blond

curls did nothing to soften the blow. He managed to get strawberry ice cream on my favorite sweater, too. My fault for wearing white to a babysitting gig, I suppose. Last time that'll happen!

"Hi, Maggie," Caroline said. "Beckett, you remember Maggie, right?"

"No," said Beckett. Then he giggled, and lucky for him his giggle was cute.

"You mean you head-butt everyone who comes through the door?" I asked, hands on my hips, playfully indignant.

"Can I come with you to walk Nofarm?" he asked.

"Oh, Maggie's not here to walk Nofarm. She's here to babysit," Caroline explained.

"No!" yelled Beckett, clinging to his mom's leg.

"We talked about this, Beckett. You knew Maggie was coming."

"Don't leave!" Beckett screamed. He held on to his mom like a clamp.

Yikes. Separation anxiety. We read about that in Babysitting 101, and not only that—I remembered the feeling from when I was little and my own parents left me for the evening. I really felt for poor Beckett. There's nothing like parents getting dressed up to go somewhere fun and abandoning you for the night with a near stranger.

It's been a couple of years since Finn and I have needed babysitters, and I must say, weekends have been a lot better since.

I bent down so Beckett and I were at eye level. "Hey, Beckett. Guess what? I brought something for you."

I pulled out a big ball of yellow clay and started to explain to him that we could build something with it. "This is just one. I've got about eight different colors and lots of—" But before I finished my sentence, Beckett grabbed the ball of clay from my hand and took off.

Caroline shook her head. "I'm so sorry, Maggie. He never behaves this way."

I tried not to laugh. "Don't worry about it," I said. "He's a three-year-old kid. He's doing exactly what he's supposed to be doing."

"I suppose," said Caroline, frowning toward the back of the apartment. "Beckett? Come out here, please."

I heard the flush of the toilet from the bathroom. Next came a clanging sort of noise. And then the water ran and ran and ran.

"Beckett!" someone screamed from the back of the apartment.

Beckett had flushed the clay down the toilet. Tried to flush it, I should say. I could tell by the sounds of the pipes that somewhere along the way it got stuck.

"Perfect, just perfect," Lisa said, clomping into the

living room in a red dress and very high patent-leather heels. She held up the dripping ball of clay. "Why would you get him this? It's not at all age-appropriate."

Caroline cringed and whispered, "I didn't."

"Then where did he get it?" asked Lisa. "Everyone knows he's not supposed to play with anything that'll fit into the toilet."

I cleared my throat and raised my hand, somewhat guiltily. "Sorry. I had no idea."

Lisa spun around and looked at me, surprised. "You're here!" she said.

"Indeed," I replied.

She smiled warmly and took a deep breath. "Thank you. That was so thoughtful, Maggie, and normally it wouldn't be an issue, but Beckett is having a hard time at the new apartment."

"I miss Brooklyn," Beckett cried.

"We still live in Brooklyn," Lisa informed him.

"No, the other Brooklyn," Beckett explained, losing patience.

"It's the same Brooklyn, sweetheart," Lisa reasoned, lowering her voice. "We're only two streets away."

"And now we have more space, and we're even closer to Prospect Park. You can see the Long Meadow from our living room," Caroline said, pointing to the back windows. "How many people can say that?"

Beckett didn't seem to care about his fabulous new view. He screwed his face up into a stubborn pout. I've seen this look on him before, and had to admire his consistency.

"Actually, before we leave, do you mind walking Nofarm?" asked Lisa. "I'd do it myself, but these heels are ridiculously uncomfortable."

"Then why are you wearing them?" asked Caroline.

"Because they look good, obviously!" Lisa winked at Caroline, who rolled her eyes.

"You're still shorter than me," she teased.

"See you guys in a few," I called as I clipped Nofarm's red leash to his purple collar and pulled him out the door. We headed down the first flight of steps without a problem. Once we got to the fourth-floor landing, though, Nofarm paused and then pulled me toward the door of apartment 4A. Then he started to whine—a painful-sounding, high-pitched noise I'd never heard from him before. Moments later I heard someone behind me.

I spun around, surprised. There in front of me were two people—father and daughter, I assumed. The girl was dressed in a Girl Scout uniform: green jumper, white shirt, sash with an impressive number of patches (if you are impressed by that kind of thing—and I am, since I never did very well as a Girl Scout). She had dark hair and heavy, severely cut bangs. She also wore slightly chunky, black-plastic-framed glasses.

She blinked at me and cringed into her father, as if she were afraid of Nofarm.

Her dad was tall and skinny with long sideburns and similar glasses. He had sleeves of tattoos on his arms: a paisley pattern around his wrists, and spiderwebs on each elbow. He wore a ski cap on his head, even though it wasn't so cold. Probably he wanted to cover up his bald spot. A lot of Park Slope dads do that—my own included.

"He must smell our cat," said the dad. "I'm Rex, by the way. And this is my daughter, Clementine."

Clementine seemed to be sucking on lemons, judging by the expression on her face.

I smiled at her, but she wouldn't meet my eye. And when I said hi, she shrank into her father even farther, as if she were trying to disappear.

I didn't take it personally, though. I figured she was just a shy kid. And scared of Nofarm, which was a little strange, considering Nofarm is the friendliest, most nonthreatening dog I know. But whatever—I tried not to judge.

"So, you must've just moved in, right?" asked Rex.

"Not exactly. Nofarm did," I said, pointing down to the dog. "I'm just the dog walker. Oh, and Beckett's new babysitter. Beckett's the three-year-old with the curly blond hair."

"Right." Rex nodded. "I haven't seen him yet, but I've definitely heard him stomping around upstairs."

"Yeah, that sounds about right." I laughed. "I'm taking care of him tonight."

"I see. Well, nice to meet you, anyway." He waved.

"You, too. Oh, I'm Maggie."

"Nice to meet you, Maggie," Rex said. As soon as he opened the door to the apartment, Clementine dashed inside.

I pulled Nofarm away, but it wasn't easy. He's strong, and he was determined, too. Whatever was behind that door, he wanted it.

Nofarm calmed down once we got outside. We walked around the block, and then I brought him back home. He paused again at the fourth-floor landing but only for a minute, because I was able to distract him with the spare dog biscuit I had in my pocket.

By the time we got to the apartment, Beckett was at the dinner table.

"We made you some mac and cheese, too," said Lisa.

"Thanks," I said, sitting down at the table. "That's so nice."

Nofarm took his place between Beckett and me and

looked back and forth from one to the other, as if trying to see who was more likely to drop food. He finally settled on Beckett, which was probably the right choice.

Lisa and Caroline went over Beckett's bedtime routine. They gave me all of their emergency phone numbers, and then put on their coats.

"Enjoy. And have fun with Beckett. We'll be back in a couple of hours." Caroline bent down and kissed Beckett on the top of his head. "Be good for Maggie, okay, sweetie?"

"Okay, but I'm always good," Beckett said with a grin.

"You sure are, sweetheart," said Lisa, giving him a final squeeze good-bye.

After they left I dug into the macaroni and cheese. It tasted good, because mac and cheese always does—but it wasn't as good as the packaged kind. It was missing the essential ingredient: powdered cheese, which is so much tastier than real cheese. And another problem? This mac and cheese had broccoli in it.

I ate a piece of it just to set an example for Beckett. And I even told him how delicious it was. "Yum!"

Beckett stared at me like he was sizing me up. And maybe seeing what he could get away with; I wasn't sure.

"Sorry about the clay," he said finally.

"That's okay," I said. "It happens. I have other stuff to play with."

"Like what?" he asked.

"Like crayons. And books—I brought my favorite book from when I was your age. It's called *In the Night Kitchen*, by Maurice Sendak."

"I have that one," said Beckett.

"Oh. Then we can read your copy, I guess."

Beckett pushed his food around on his plate.

"So, you don't like living here?"

Beckett didn't answer me.

"Is that a no?" I asked.

"Yeah. I don't like it," he mumbled.

"How come?" I asked.

He looked up at me and said, "I'm finished with my dinner."

"Okay." I jumped up and grabbed both of our bowls and put them in the kitchen sink. Then I went back to the dining room where Beckett still sat with his legs swinging back and forth, feet far from the sleek hardwood floor.

"Um, want to show me your room?"

Beckett shrugged again.

I grinned at him. "You like to shrug."

He started to shrug again but stopped and giggled.

I wiggled my eyebrows at him.

"How do you feel about LEGOs?" I asked.

"Good." He nodded. "I like them."

"Me, too," I said. "Want to build a tower?"

"Yeah." Beckett scrambled to his feet, lugged over a huge bag of LEGOs, and dumped them in the middle of the living room.

After building a tower, a parking garage, and a space station, he showed me his train tracks. Then we raced Matchbox cars across the living-room floor. And then it was seven o'clock—bedtime.

"Okay, time to brush your teeth," I said.

"I brushed them this morning," Beckett said.

"That's good," I said. "It's time to do it again."

"Okay, fine," Beckett mumbled resignedly as he shuffled his feet toward the bathroom.

I followed him in and found eight toothbrushes sticking out of a Buzz Lightyear cup. "These are all yours?" I asked.

"Yup," Beckett said.

"Which one do you want to use?" I asked.

He picked out the red one and handed it to me. I added some strawberry-flavored organic toothpaste and helped him brush his little teeth. Then we picked out some books. He didn't want to read the one I brought, so we settled on *Goodnight Moon*, something about a pigeon, and something about John Coltrane called

*Before John Was a Jazz Giant*. Cool pictures and cool story. I thought, This babysitting gig is fun. I could get used to it.

After we finished with the three books, I said, "Time for bed," and tucked Beckett in.

"Your sheets match your pajamas," I said, taking in the moon and stars and rocket ships. "You could get lost in here, you blend in so well."

Beckett giggled.

"Good night," I said.

When I tried to leave, he grabbed my arm. "Can you open my closet door?" he asked.

"You want the door open?" I said.

He nodded. This surprised me, because when I was little, Finn and I couldn't close our eyes and get comfortable if the closet door was open even a crack. We thought monsters lived there—weird creatures with pointy teeth and hairy arms. Yet somehow, we also believed that the closet door was a powerful barrier, like even the scariest monsters wouldn't be able to open a simple door.

"Why do you want me to open the door?" I asked.

"Because Margaret only visits me when the door is open," he replied.

Chills ran up and down my spine. My shoulders shook involuntarily. I tried not to act bothered, because

I didn't want to make Beckett nervous—Which is funny, because even as I thought this I noticed he was perfectly calm and relaxed. I was the one who felt about ready to jump out of my own skin.

"Who did you say you want to visit?" I asked Beckett.

"Margaret," he said.

"And who's Margaret?" I asked carefully. Even though I'd asked Beckett the question, I had the feeling that I didn't actually want to hear his answer.

"She's my friend," he said simply as he rearranged his stuffed animals around him on the bed.

I felt panicked for a moment. But I told myself to calm down, because there had to be a reasonable explanation.

"Does Margaret go to school with you?" I asked.

"No, she's old," said Beckett. "Her skin is so white she's see-through."

"You mean, like a—" I stopped myself. I didn't want to say "ghost." Didn't want to introduce the idea of one.

Beckett had to be making things up. The kid had an active imagination. He must've heard other people talking about Margaret. He probably remembered her name and turned her into his imaginary friend.

I turned to the closet and raised my voice. "Hi, Margaret. I'm Maggie Brooklyn, Beckett's babysitter. It's nice to meet you."

"Who are you talking to?" asked Beckett.

"Your imaginary friend, Margaret," I said, feeling kind of silly. I waved, but this made me feel even more ridiculous.

Clearly Beckett was not fooled. He sighed. "She's not here yet."

"Oh," I said.

"And she's real." Beckett stared at me intensely, and somehow I knew the kid truly believed what he was saying.

"Right," I said, backing away from his bed. "Sorry about that. I thought I saw her, but I guess not. Tell her I say hi, if you happen to see her. Okay?"

"Sure," said Beckett.

I went to leave his room, but before I made it out he yelled at me.

"You forgot the closet!"

"Right. Sorry." I opened it up for him, and he lay back down and stared at the ceiling.

I paused at the door and asked, "Is she here yet?"

"Nope," said Beckett.

"Well, tell her I say hello," I said again and left Beckett in his room, to his imaginary friend, because Margaret had to be imaginary.

There is no such thing as ghosts.

There is no such thing as ghosts.

There's just not.

Except the more I repeated this, the less convinced I became.

Maybe I just needed a distraction, I thought, flopping down on the living room couch and opening up my math book. I was just getting into the first problem when suddenly I heard something from the back of the apartment—a muffled sort of dripping. I jumped up and checked on Beckett through the crack in his bedroom door. He was staring at the ceiling with his eyes wide open.

But the sound wasn't coming from his room.

I tiptoed into his moms' room. In their bathroom, the sink was dripping. I tightened the faucet, then jumped at the sight of myself in the mirror. They'd already replaced the giant mirror that had shattered; it was propped up on the wall opposite their bed.

I moved closer and studied myself.

I looked freaked out, which made me feel silly. Because what did I have to worry about? I'm twelve years old. I have a successful dog-walking business. I've solved a bunch of mysteries.

And I don't believe in ghosts.

Because they do not exist.

Period.

It's a fact.

Of course, it was also a fact that I was shivering.

But this had to be because it was chilly in Beckett's apartment.

I checked the thermostat. It read seventy-three degrees. The heat was blasting, and I was still wearing my thick wool sweater.

When I got back to the living room the sun had set, so the room was dark. I flicked on the light switch, but nothing happened. There was a reading light on the table by the couch, and I tried to turn it on. But the bulb was out there, too.

No reason to panic, though, because this was not a creepy apartment. I reminded myself that I was in Park Slope, a mere three blocks away from the apartment where I've lived for my entire life. I've passed by this building thousands of times, probably, and never even gave it a second look.

I turned on the kitchen light, which cast a glow in the living room. It wasn't enough light to read by, though.

I wished I'd brought a flashlight, or this headlamp I got the one time I went camping.

It didn't help that Nofarm was acting so strange—unsettled and completely stressed out. He kept randomly barking at the walls and scratching at the floorboards, as though there was some sort of—I don't know—otherwordly and invisible presence there. Except that was impossible.

But maybe I was thinking about things too much. Perhaps all I needed was a distraction. Homework, for instance; I still had plenty of it.

For my history paper I planned on going to the library, but I figured the Internet was a good place to start. Once I googled Jonas Adams, I would be able to dispel the entire haunted-mansion myth. The whole story had to be some crazy urban legend, probably not even popular enough for anyone to write about.

But unfortunately what I found verified everything Milo had said.

A few websites mentioned Jonas Adams and his chocolate empire—back then he was called Brooklyn's King of Chocolate. Every site mentioned the gigantic mansion he built next to his factory, and the freak accident that took the life of a poor Irish servant named Margaret.

But could her ghost be haunting Beckett? And if so, why wasn't he scared?

The next time I checked on Beckett he turned to me and asked what I wanted. "Why do you keep coming in here?" he said.

"I don't know," I said. "This is my first time babysitting, so I figured I should check up on you."

"Most babysitters don't do that," said Beckett.

"Oh," I said. For a moment it kind of felt like he was

taking care of me. I coughed and stood up straighter. "Do you need anything? A glass of water?" I wasn't about to admit to a three-year-old that hanging out at his house was creeping me out—or that I felt safer with him than I did out in the living room by myself.

"No," he said.

"Okay. Let me know if you do."

"Okay," said Beckett.

"Um, is Margaret here?"

"Do you see her?" he asked, as if I were stupid.

"I don't see her," I said, looking around the room. "But I thought she might be invisible or something."

"She's not invisible," Beckett told me.

"Okay, then."

As I left his room I felt silly for acting nervous, because I'm supposed to be the responsible babysitter. That means if there is a ghost—if the building is truly haunted—it's my job to protect Beckett. Of course, my babysitter training course covered choking, fires, break-ins, and other emergencies, but the instructor never talked about what to do in case of a ghost . . .

I looked out the window. Prospect Park stretched out below, peaceful and green. I looked up at the full moon. *A full moon. Great.* That was just the kind of creepy detail I didn't want to notice.

I sat back down on the living-room couch and tried

to focus on my math homework. But I found it impossible. My mind kept drifting back to the website dedicated to the haunted mansion. I went back to the computer and checked again.

Everything Milo had told me about was there. And a whole lot more.

I read all about Margaret. She was the only daughter of a family of potato farmers. She wrote home to her family every single week. She liked to sing. Sure, she worked as a maid, but she dreamed of being a nurse. She had just enrolled in classes at Brooklyn College, and was supposed to start in the fall. She had a fiancé in Ireland, too, a boy named Michael. He was saving up money to make passage to the United States.

She probably came in to the United States via Ellis Island, where most immigrants first set foot on American soil. We'd studied Ellis Island in history last year, so I had an idea of what Margaret's experience must've been like. I closed my eyes and tried to picture her stepping off the boat and seeing New York for the first time. All the hustle and bustle, the cars and people and new smells and sounds and sights: America—the land of opportunity, the place where good things were supposed to happen. I'll bet Margaret was nervous, but I'm sure she never imagined her life would soon be ending, or that her ending would involve being trapped in some rich guy's elevator.

Suddenly I heard a strange scraping noise. I looked up, and in the semidarkness saw something move.

At first I feared it was a mouse, but mice don't have sharp, gleaming edges.

Once my eyes adjusted, I saw it was Beckett's remote-control car traveling slowly across the floor—all by itself.

# Chapter 13

• • •

The car glided smoothly, as though propelled by an invisible hand.

A ghost hand.

I looked across the living room at Beckett's door, which stood slightly ajar. Then I noticed the remote control next to me on the table. I picked it up, thinking maybe I'd accidentally triggered it somehow—but the entire remote felt suspiciously light. I turned it over and opened the battery compartment. The *empty* battery compartment.

There were no batteries in the remote.

I yelled and threw it across the room, then ducked under the afghan on the couch. As if a bunch of yarn could protect me. Yarn filled with dust, I realized as I immediately sneezed. I threw off the afghan and tried not to panic, because I was supposed to be the responsible babysitter. I had a job to do: protect Beckett. But how could I protect him from something that didn't exist?

I stared at the car, now sitting in the middle of the living room, a good three feet away.

*Okay,* I told myself. *That did not just happen.* I must've imagined the whole incident. Except here's the thing: I knew I didn't.

The car had been on one side of the room, and it drove to the other side of the room—all by itself.

The next time I checked on Beckett he was asleep, so I closed his door.

I turned on the hall light. And the fancy crystal chandelier in the dining room, and every other working light source I could find in the entire house, except for those in Beckett's and his moms' rooms.

Not knowing what to do with myself next, I walked into the kitchen and peeked into every single cabinet. I found dishes, wineglasses, regular glasses, and the food pantry. I munched a handful of baked potato chips, then ate some mixed nuts. Then I wandered back into the living room and turned on the TV, figuring I could use a distraction. But guess what was playing? *Friday the 13th.*

Because tonight was the thirteenth of the month. Not Friday, but still; thirteen is an unlucky number any day of the week.

I turned off the TV and opened my book, thinking I'd do some English homework. Except my assignment was to answer questions about "The Raven," by Edgar Allan Poe. The poem starts like this: *Once upon a midnight dreary, while I pondered, weak and weary.* I slammed the book shut, because that opening line sounded way too creepy for tonight. Then I read about the poem online. It turned out "The Raven" was about a talking bird and a man grieving over the death of his girlfriend. Gah! That's the absolute *worst* poem I could read right then. It was like I was being stalked by spooky stuff.

I went back to math, because there's nothing scary about numbers.

After I finished the assignment I looked at my watch. I'd been taking care of Beckett for over three hours now. Lisa and Caroline were only going out to dinner, as far as I knew. That's what they'd told me, anyway; they also said they'd only be gone for a couple of hours—meaning two—so where were they?

How long did dinner take?

What if they didn't come back?

What if their plan all along was to ditch Beckett with the unassuming and inexperienced babysitter and hightail it out of town and away from their haunted house?

At least they knew I would take good care of Nofarm.

I wasn't thinking straight. No way would they abandon Beckett. Why would I even think such a crazy thing? This house was making me lose my mind!

I wandered around the apartment again, opening all the doors that had been closed, including Beckett's. I found him asleep on top of his spaceship quilt, half his curls smushed against his pillow.

When I glanced at the closet in his room, I jumped at the sight of myself. Apparently the back wall was covered in mirrors that I somehow hadn't noticed before.

I hurried back to the living room, flopped down on the couch, picked up my phone, and texted Sonya.

What r u doing?

Playing hearts with Felicity. U?

Babysitting for Beckett

In the haunted house?

It's not haunted.

R u sure?

Not funny.

I wasn't kidding. Careful of Mindy!

Margaret! If you must tease me at least get the ghost's name right

Sorry dude.

I tossed my phone into my bag, wishing I could call Milo, but he already owed me too many calls. Anyway, what would I tell him—*I think you were right about the ghost, and now I'm stuck here. Please help me*? I didn't need anyone to rescue me. Anyway, based on Milo's initial reaction to this house, I'm sure he would never set foot inside. Maybe it was better that we weren't speaking at the moment. Maybe if I told him where I was, what had happened, and how scared I was, he'd say I told you so.

Not that any of this mattered, because calling Milo was not an option. I'd already tried to get in touch with him too many times, so now I had to wait.

I looked around the apartment, wondering what to do. A fresh copy of the *New York Times* sat on Lisa and

Caroline's coffee table. The story on the front page was about Amtrak's terrible safety record and their attempts to cover it up. It made me remember something my grandmother once told me: reading the *New York Times* cover to cover for a year would make me smarter than studying at any university. This always seemed like the kind of great advice I'd never actually follow. But tonight I had a change of heart. Tonight I felt like I may as well try.

I picked up the paper and began reading. And the next thing I knew, someone's hand was on my shoulder.

I opened my eyes, saw someone standing right in front of me, and screamed.

"Ah! What's going on?" I asked, scrambling to my feet.

"It's okay. It's just us," said Caroline as she took off her jacket and hung it in the closet by the front door. "You dozed off."

"Oh, right. Sorry," I said, realizing it was Beckett's parents and not the ghost of Margaret in front of me. "I can't believe I fell asleep on the job. I've never done that before. I mean, I've never babysat before, either, but I'm sure I'll never do it again. Fall asleep, I mean. Not babysit. I checked on Beckett six times, and he's always been okay. Let me check on him now."

"It's okay. We just did," said Lisa. "Beckett is fine."

"I'm so sorry," I said again.

"Don't be. We should be apologizing to you because it's so late. We weren't expecting to be gone for so long, but there was over an hour wait for a table at al di la," Caroline explained. "I guess we should've called."

Lisa sank down into an easy chair and kicked off her heels. "How was he?" she asked as she rubbed her left foot.

"Beckett? He was great. We made a tower out of LEGOs and read a bunch of books, and he went to bed. Oh—this was weird. He wanted the closet door open. He kept talking about someone named Margaret visiting him . . ."

Lisa and Caroline glanced at each other, and their expressions told me they weren't surprised by my news. Neither of them seemed willing to talk about it, though.

"So, what's up with that?" I asked.

"We should've mentioned Margaret. She's his imaginary friend," said Caroline. "Just like the ghost who supposedly haunts this place. I'm guessing he heard someone talk about her and invented his own Margaret character."

"Ha!" I forced a laugh, but it sounded choked. "That's what I figured, but I just wanted to make sure he's not being visited by the actual ghost."

Lisa and Caroline laughed, too. "Nope. We haven't seen any ghosts around."

"Good," I said. "But have you noticed all the creepy noises in the building? I can see why people think it's haunted."

"I know it's got that reputation, but trust me, it's just an old house," said Caroline. "That's what happens. Buildings are alive; they have their own quirks and personalities, in a sense. The pipes clang when the heat goes on, and wood expands and contracts with the weather. Mortar crumbles. Foundations shift over time. Basically, the building is still settling. It always will be, to some degree, and sometimes that produces strange noises."

This made sense, but it didn't exactly ease my mind. I was already worried about Margaret the ghost—but now I had to worry about the building, too? How much more stress could I handle?

Let me answer that question for you: not much! I was itching to get out of the apartment—the whole building, even. At this point, I'd avoid the entire block if I could. Because now that I was fully awake, I remembered why I was so freaked out in the first place. "The remote control car started working on its own," I blurted out.

Both Lisa and Caroline cracked up, which was not the reaction I was expecting.

"I'm sorry," said Caroline, "but you ought to have seen your face just now. And I shouldn't laugh, because I probably had the same reaction when it happened to me the first time last week."

"It's happened to you more than once?" I asked.

"We should've warned you," said Caroline. "It's because the car runs on the same frequency as our neighbor's remote control, so anytime they turn on the TV next door, the car shifts a little."

"But it didn't just shift a little bit," I said, "it moved at least three feet."

"That's probably because the floor is slanted," said Lisa. To demonstrate, she went to Beckett's toy box, pulled out a Matchbox car, and placed it in the corner of the room. She lifted her hand gently, and the car rolled all the way across the floor as if propelled by an invisible hand.

I sighed in relief and giggled out of nervousness all at the same time. "I *so* wish I had known that two hours ago," I told them.

"Sorry," said Lisa. "We were in such a rush to get out of here we forgot to mention it."

"I didn't even think it would come up," said Caroline. "But other than that, I'm so happy everything went well. Beckett loves you, I can tell. So will you babysit again? It would help us out a lot."

I didn't know what to say at first. I couldn't exactly admit that their apartment creeped me out—not when I didn't believe in ghosts.

"Know what?" I said. "I have a twin brother named Finn, and he's trying to break into the business. So could we maybe babysit together next time? He's amazing with kids, and super sweet, too."

"Okay," said Lisa. "That works for us. And maybe you two can keep each other awake."

"Right." I cringed. "So sorry about that!"

"I'm kidding," Lisa said as she looked down at her phone and pressed some buttons, pulling up her calendar. "How about Friday night?"

"You mean next weekend?" I asked. "As in, six days from now?"

"Yes. Is that okay?" asked Lisa. "My company is hosting a benefit downtown, and I really need to show my face."

I felt totally put on the spot. If I said no, I'd seem like a wimp. But if I said yes, I'd be stuck babysitting. Of course, maybe it wouldn't be so bad with Finn there. And he did need the money. And once I got around to having Mom sign my test, she'd probably never let me babysit again anyway. So maybe I should just do it while I still had the opportunity. "Sure," I said softly. "Friday works for me."

"That's wonderful," said Caroline. "Six forty-five okay?"

"Yup." I nodded, reasoning to myself that I could always text them tomorrow and cancel.

If I wanted to admit to the world that I was a big, fat, scaredy-cat.

# Chapter 14

• • •

A few days later, I stopped by Sonya's Sweets after school. Sonya's mom had finally gotten around to uploading the pictures from the opening day onto her laptop.

"I'm sorry it took so long," she said. "We couldn't find the right cable. Somehow, it ended up in the recycling bag and almost got thrown away. Things are so crazy these days."

"It's fine. Don't worry about it." I wished I had more words of reassurance for Ricki, but the truth was, I had no idea how I was going to solve this mystery, and I didn't want to lie about that.

We sat in the back booth—the same one where I'd had my first double date. But we could've parked ourselves anywhere, since there were only a few customers in the entire shop. Joshua was behind the counter giving Sonya a lesson on frosting cakes. Everything seemed to be running smoothly, but Ricki kept looking up to survey the store, as if she expected something horrible to happen at any moment. I guess that made sense, since so many things had gone wrong already; but still, her skittishness made me sad.

Once the pictures were finally ready to look at, Ricki pressed some buttons and frowned down at her computer. "Hold on one second," she said. "I always forget which button to press to get from one image to the next. They say these new computers are completely intuitive, but I still have trouble."

"Don't worry about it," I said as I carefully reached over and pressed the right button.

"Thank you," Ricki said.

I shrugged. Old people can be funny about technology, and Ricki had pretty good excuses for not being clearheaded enough to figure things out at the moment. Sonya had reminded me again of how stressed out her mom was about the failing business, but of course I didn't bring any of that up.

Ricki shifted over to make room so I could sit in front of the computer. Then we looked through the pictures together.

Many of them were taken before the store even opened. They featured Sonya and her mom and dad and

Felicity standing in front of the shop. The beautiful picture window was in full view to their right—all those glittering food characters dancing around, sweet and cheerful.

Sonya's entire family wore white paper soda-jerk hats and goofy grins. Their arms were wrapped around each other, and their eyes shined bright with excitement.

The next few shots featured everyone bustling around inside, getting ready. Then finally I got to the images from the grand opening.

"He was our first customer," said Ricki, pointing to the close-up of a stunned man with a mustache. "He wasn't expecting the camera in his face when he walked in, I guess."

As I progressed through the pictures, the store got more and more crowded. The place was packed with neighborhood moms and dads and babies, enough strollers to trip over, and kids of all ages. Everyone looked happy and excited about the new place, which made sense, because who doesn't love dessert? It was impossible to believe that Sonya's Sweets could be anything but a huge success. If only Ricki could wait until the kinks got straightened out. If only I could figure out who was behind all of the mayhem!

Eventually I got to the pictures of myself with Milo, Finn, and Lulu. In the first one, Finn and Lulu were holding hands. Milo was glancing at me, and I was looking down, smiling about some joke he'd made.

Back when we were a happy couple. Back when we were a couple, period. We still hadn't spoken since our fight. Last Sunday I broke down and called his actual house. His grandma, Valerie, answered the phone. She told me Milo was fine but he couldn't talk. Valerie seemed to feel bad, like she wished she could say more, but she didn't. And as relieved as I was to hear he was okay, the entire situation—and Milo's behavior in particular—left me feeling so frustrated. I didn't even know whether I wanted to be his girlfriend anymore, but it's not like I could talk to his grandma about that.

"I didn't even realize you took that picture," I said, pointing to the image of Milo and me. What I didn't say was, *I wonder if we'll ever get back to that sweet, happy place.*

Ricki squinted at the computer. "Joshua must've taken it. He took over as store photographer and got sneaky, taking a bunch of candid shots. Did you find some sort of clue?"

"No, sorry," I said as I continued scrolling. "I got distracted." There were a few more shots of me and Milo, Lulu, and Finn, but none were as great as that very first image.

Joshua must've gotten bored of taking pictures of

people entering the store, because the next ten shots were of Felicity.

I saw, in order, the following:

1) Felicity scooping ice cream and getting the sleeve of her sweater caught in the tub of strawberry.
2) Felicity cleaning her sweater at the sink in the back room.
3) Felicity reattempting to scoop the ice cream but accidentally dropping it on the floor.
4) Felicity kicking the dropped scoop of melted ice cream underneath the counter as she looked over her shoulder to make sure nobody else could see. (Obviously she remained oblivious to the fact that Joshua had his zoom lens focused on her.)
5) Felicity successfully presenting a young soccer player with two scoops of ice cream.
6) Felicity licking some extra vanilla ice cream off her wrist.
7) Felicity hiding under the counter, texting.
8) Felicity looking up suspiciously, as if she sensed she might not be alone.
9) Felicity staring straight at the camera, shocked and annoyed.

10) Someone's hand over the lens—probably Felicity's.

After the Felicity show, the subject matter turned back to the actual soda fountain opening. Eventually I stopped flipping through the photos, because I saw someone who looked strangely familiar. She was on the young side—maybe eight or nine—and she wore dark sunglasses and jeans and a big flannel shirt. She was with an older woman who seemed to be her mom. And she leaned into her in a familiar way.

"Do you know who that is?" I asked Ricki.

Ricki considered the photo. "No idea," she told me.

I stared at the picture. I'd seen the girl somewhere recently; I just couldn't remember where. Perhaps she was a neighborhood kid I'd passed on the street. Or maybe there was more to her story. I had the feeling that her presence at the store was significant, somehow, but I couldn't say for sure, and I couldn't say why.

Glancing at my watch, I saw it was getting late, and I still had three dogs to walk before dark.

"Do you mind if I put these on Flickr so I can take a look at them later?" I asked.

"If you know how to do that, then please be my guest," said Ricki.

I was just finishing when Finn walked into the store and waved to me.

"What's up, bro?" I asked.

"I had some time and thought I'd walk some dogs with you today," he said.

"You mean you're not here for the food?" asked Ricki. "I promise you we worked out the problem with the pies."

"And I'm sure they're delicious," said Finn. "I'll definitely try one next time. But I just wolfed down two slices from Pizza Den and I'm feeling kind of queasy."

"Hold on just a second," I said as I punched in the last few bits of information and then closed Ricki's laptop. "Okay, let's go."

As soon as we made it outside, Finn said, "So, which dog do you walk first?"

"It depends," I said. "Usually I start with Bean. She's the toughest dog, so I like getting her out of the way. But Nofarm's been kinda challenging lately, too."

"Well, I'll just follow you," said Finn. He shoved his hands in his pockets and looked at the ground as we walked.

"So why are you really here?" I asked.

"What do you mean?" asked Finn.

"Come on," I said. "I've been walking dogs for months, and you've never wanted to tag along before. So what's the deal? Do you need to borrow money or something? I already lined up a great babysitting gig for us for this weekend."

"Yeah, in a haunted mansion!" said Finn.

"It's not haunted," I insisted. "It's just old."

"I know, I'm just teasing," said Finn. "And I'm not asking for money. I'm trying to help you."

"With dog walking?" I asked. "I've been doing pretty well on my own."

"I mean the Milo situation," said Finn. "I talked to him."

I stopped dead in my tracks. "You what?" I asked.

"Don't yell," he said.

"Did I yell? Sorry. I meant to say, are you crazy?" I socked Finn on the shoulder. I couldn't help myself. "Why would you talk to my boyfriend?"

"He's not just your boyfriend," said Finn, "he's my friend, too. And you're my sister. And he's not talking to you, and I see what it's doing to you and I want to know why."

"So you just called him and asked him why he won't return my calls?" I asked.

"Please give me some credit, Mags. I was much more subtle. I called to tell him about the history homework, and then I asked him where he's been."

"And what did he say?"

"He's been sick, but it's nothing serious—just a bad case of food poisoning. There's other stuff going on, too, I think. But he didn't go into details. He brought you up, though. He said he owed you a call, and you guys needed to talk."

This was all very interesting. I had a bunch of questions for Finn, but before I managed to formulate my first one, I noticed something odd.

Someone was walking down the street with an entire grocery cart filled with Girl Scout cookies. And here's the weirdest part about it: she wasn't even a Girl Scout. She was a grown-up. A grown-up dressed all in black with a giant, floppy red sunhat on her head.

"Hey," I whispered, elbowing Finn.

"Ouch," he said, rubbing his arm.

"Too hard?" I asked. "Sorry. But see that lady over there? We've got to follow her."

"Wait, why?" Finn asked, jogging to catch up with me.

"She's our new lead," I said. I didn't have time to explain any more because she was getting away.

The woman took long strides, pulling her grocery cart behind her with one hand as the other swung back and forth. Finn and I were right on her heels, following her for two blocks and then around the corner.

Soon, though, she looked over her shoulder. I tried to duck behind a parked car and pull Finn along with me, but I wasn't fast enough.

Spotting us, she came marching over, asking, "What do you think you're doing?"

My first instinct was to run, and I could tell Finn wanted to scram, too, because he grabbed my hand and started tugging me away. But here's the thing: we weren't doing anything wrong. We are allowed to walk down whatever street we want to, and I was completely ready to tell her so.

"Are you talking to me?" I asked in my most innocent tone of voice.

"Yeah," she said, pretty aggressively. "What's your deal?"

I looked to Finn, who'd gone a little pale. "My deal?" I asked.

"Why are you two following me?" She took off her sunglasses to reveal piercing blue eyes that stared me down, questioning. "And how come you two look so much alike?"

"We're twins," I told her.

"Yeah," said Finn, finally speaking up. "And we're wondering what you're doing with all those cookies, because we've got a hankering for some. Think you could sell us a box?"

I grinned at Finn, thrilled that he'd thought of a cover story. My brother surprised me sometimes.

"Oh, of course," said the woman, relaxing a bit. "I

should've known I'd get a lot of attention with all my cookies."

"They're all for you?" I asked.

"Sure," said the woman. "I'm not going to eat them, but I need them for my new piece. I'm a conceptual artist; I'm working on a new sculpture having to do with the state of girlhood in the modern era."

"Huh?" asked Finn. I had to agree with him.

The woman tried to explain. "Basically, I'm constructing a Girl Scout out of Girl Scout cookie boxes."

"Why?" asked Finn.

"Because it's art," she said. "My name is Gabby, by the way. I'd shake your hand, if I could."

I looked down. I hadn't noticed before, but her entire forearm was encased in a fiberglass cast. "Must be hard to work with that," I said.

"It hasn't been easy, but I manage. It's really hard to write, though. I'm stuck writing with my left hand, which hasn't been working out so well. I'm not exactly ambidextrous."

"Bummer," said Finn.

"Hey, where did you get all those boxes, anyway?" I asked.

"Girl Scout troop number forty-five," Gabby told me. "They're the top-selling troop in town. Those girls are fierce."

"Do you know any of the Girl Scouts personally?" I asked. "Because we'd really like to buy some."

"Sure," said Gabby. "Let me get the number for you." She pulled out her phone and searched awkwardly for the information, with the fingers of her left hand.

"What happened to your arm?" I asked.

"Bicycle accident in the park," said Gabby. "It happened last month. Pretty brutal, too. You know how there are crosswalks and traffic signals and sometimes cyclists have the right-of-way?"

"Yup," I said with a nod.

"Well, some of your neighbors don't, apparently. I was a part of a ten-bike crash last Saturday."

"Yikes, that sounds scary," I said.

"Oh, it was," said Gabby. "But it could've been worse. Everyone had their helmets on, luckily. A few of us ended up at the hospital with broken bones. But I get the cast off in two short weeks. No need to worry, however. My work hasn't suffered too much. At least not according to the *New York Times*. I had a review of my last show in the arts section."

"That's great."

She pulled some flyers out of her oversize pocket with her good hand. "You should stop by the gallery. You're never too young to take an interest in art."

"Um, okay," I said, staring down at the flyer, which featured a sculpture of a dog made out of what looked like dog biscuits.

"That one is cool," I said, pointing. "Where is it?"

"Nowhere," said Gabby. "It used to be on display in a gallery in DUMBO, but it got devoured because I released a pack of dogs inside. I got most of it on video, though. You can find it on YouTube if you look."

"Are you going to bring in a pack of wild Girl Scouts to eat your next sculpture?" Finn asked.

"Huh," said Gabby, taking his question a little too seriously. "That's not a bad idea. I may use that. Thanks."

Finn and I looked at each other, both wondering whether Gabby was serious, and silently agreeing not to ask.

"Anyway, here's Clementine's number," said Gabby, handing me a slip of paper. "She's the troop leader."

"Clementine?" I asked. "Is she the Girl Scout who lives at the corner of Eighth Avenue and Carroll Street?"

"Yeah—Rex's daughter," said Gabby.

"I just met them last week," I said. "I walk their neighbor's dog."

"Small world. Rex and I went to college together. I haven't talked to him in ages."

"Then how did you end up buying cookies from his daughter?" Finn asked.

“That girl is wily. She hacked into his Facebook account to find new customers.”

“That’s pretty serious,” I said.

“No kidding. In fact, she’s my inspiration for this whole project.”

“Good luck with that,” I said. “Nice meeting you, Gabby.”

“Same here.” Gabby saluted us with her cast-encased right arm and went on her way, pulling her cart behind her.

“That was close,” Finn said, once we were out of earshot. “She seemed really mad at first.”

“Guess I have to work on my surveillance skills,” I said. “But we got some good intel.”

“You think?” he asked. “Please explain.”

“I can’t yet. I’m still trying to puzzle everything out. I have a hunch, but it’s too soon to talk.”

Just then Finn ran into his buddy Red, and the two of them went off to try out some new video game.

After walking Bean, Dog-Milo, and Nofarm, I went home and picked up my phone. Texting Milo seemed safer than calling, but what did I have to say? *I talked to Finn. Glad you are okay. But how come you still won’t speak to me?*

I put my phone away and opened up my laptop instead, deciding to take another look at the pictures from the grand opening.

Girl Scout cookies were on my mind in a major way, and Girl Scouts, too. And that's when I realized something. The girl in the picture from the opening? The one who looked so familiar? She was Clementine, the Girl Scout who lived downstairs from Beckett. The one Gabby described as ruthless. It made me wonder, could she be messing with the store because she doesn't want the competition?

It certainly made sense for her to have written the note. But how would she have shattered the window if she was inside the store? Was she working with someone else? And if so, who?

# Chapter 15

• • •

I still wasn't positive about who to blame for the sabotage at Sonya's Sweets, but something told me that talking to Clementine would give me some answers.

That's why I headed over to the mansion early on Friday night, so I could drop by for a chat.

Luckily for me, they were home. Clementine's dad, Rex, answered the door right away, and he remembered me from last week.

"Hi," he said, smiling at me. "You're Nofarm's dog walker. Right?"

"Yup. That's me. Maggie Brooklyn."

He grinned. "Maggie Brooklyn. Great name. What can I do for you?"

"Um, I was wondering whether your daughter, Clementine, was home. I have some Girl-Scout-cookie-related questions for her."

Rex nodded. “You’ve definitely come to the right apartment for that. I’m sure Clementine would be happy to speak with you. She’s an expert in cookie sales. Hold on a second. Clementine!” he called.

No one answered.

Rex said, “I’ll be right back,” and headed for the back of the apartment.

Since the door was open, I stepped inside. Then I heard mumbling from another room.

“But I don’t want to,” Clementine said.

“Come on, Clem. It’s nice that someone came to see you,” her dad replied.

“Why are you making me seem like a loser with no friends?” she asked.

“I’m not. I’m just saying, ever since Mom’s been away you’ve hardly been out of your room, and now you have the chance to talk to—”

“Oh my gosh. My own father thinks I’m a loser with no friends. I am *fine* without Mom. She can *move* to London for all I care!”

“She’s only working there for a few more weeks. I know it’s been hard, but—”

“I told you, I’m fine!”

From these snippets of conversation, it seemed pretty obvious that Clementine had no interest in talking to me. I wondered if her mom had been with her at the opening. The older woman in the picture, the one she was leaning into, certainly looked like her. I'd have to ask, once they finished fighting.

A minute later Clementine came marching toward the front door, with her father right behind her. He wasn't exactly pushing her, but he may as well have been, from the sour-lemon look on Clementine's face.

"Who are you?" she asked.

I smiled brightly. "I'm Maggie Brooklyn. Remember? We met the other day, with your dad. I walk the dog upstairs. And I take care of Beckett sometimes. And you're just the person I wanted to see."

"I know all about Beckett," Clementine grumbled. "His room is right above mine, and he dropped a bag of marbles on his floor at six o'clock this morning."

"Yeah, that sounds about right." I laughed, but Clementine didn't.

"Let's not complain about Beckett," said Rex, putting his arm around Clementine. "You were three once, too. Remember?"

"Not really," Clementine grumbled.

Rex winked at me, as if we were all in on some hilarious joke.

"I need to head to the bodega and pick up some groceries for dinner. Okay if I leave you two here?" Rex asked, grabbing his coat off the rack by the door and slipping into it.

"It's fine with me," I said.

"Me, too," said Clementine.

"Great. See you in ten." Rex kissed his daughter on her forehead and waved good-bye to me.

As nice as it was to have someone cheerful in the apartment, I was glad Rex had gone. I wanted to speak with Clementine alone, because we had a lot of ground to cover.

"Mind if I ask you a few questions?" I asked.

Clementine shrugged noncommittally.

"Great," I said. "I'm kind of in the middle of a couple of things, and I could really use your help."

"With what?" Clementine asked suspiciously.

I could see her getting defensive, so I decided not to bring up Sonya's Sweets right away. Instead I asked her about the ghost of Margaret. "I don't want to freak you out or anything, but have you ever heard the rumors that your house is haunted?"

Clementine rolled her eyes and let out a heavy sigh. "Of course I know about the haunted house. I've lived here, like, forever."

I'd felt silly before, but Clementine's reaction made me feel absolutely ridiculous. "So what do you think?" I asked. "Is there any truth to the rumors?"

"Of course not," said Clementine.

"So you haven't seen any ghosts?" I asked.

"Are you serious?"

"I only ask because I'm worried about Beckett," I said, bluffing only slightly. "He thinks this ghost—Margaret—comes to visit him at night. And since his room is directly above yours, well . . . I was just wondering whether you've seen anything."

"Nope," said Clementine.

"Mind if I take a look out your window?" I asked. "Just so I can reassure Beckett's parents."

Clementine sighed and said, "Fine. Come on in."

I followed her into the living room. The layout of the apartment seemed to be exactly the same as the Jones's place, except the furniture was older and looked more lived-in. On the living-room wall was an electric guitar, hung as though it were a painting.

"That's cool," I said.

Clementine gazed up at the guitar and said, "My dad collects them. That was his first Stratocaster; he doesn't want to play it anymore because it's too valuable or something."

"Is your room back here?" I asked, pointing to the door off the living room.

"How'd you know that?" she asked suspiciously.

"Your apartment looks just like Beckett's family's place, and his bedroom is over there," I explained.

"Oh," said Clementine. "Yes. Follow me."

The first thing I noticed about Clementine's room

was the color. All four walls were painted green. Not a soothing minty green or a rich dark shade—I'm talking primary-color bright green, like a Girl Scout uniform.

The next thing that struck me was the view. Clementine's bedroom window looked out onto my friend Beatrix's building. And the buildings were so close together that I could actually see what was going on in the apartment next door. An older kid was at his desk, on a computer doing homework, maybe, or looking at Instagram or something. I couldn't see his computer screen, but he was so close I could tell he had bushy eyebrows and a picture of John Lennon on his shirt. That's how close I was; I felt like I could reach out and touch the window next door.

"See anything interesting?" Clementine asked.

I spun around. "That building is so close to this one!" I said, gesturing across the street.

"I know," said Clementine. "That's why I always make sure to close the curtains at night, because I don't want anyone peeking in."

"That's probably a good idea," I said, looking around.

Clementine's room was the neatest room I'd ever seen for a kid. Her bed was made and her green blanket was tucked in, hospital-corner style. Her desk was covered with notebooks arranged at perfect right angles. There were some highlighters in her pencil cup—pink, green, yellow, and blue, each spaced about an inch apart, almost as if she'd measured them.

A blue highlighter—with the same color ink as the note on the back of the box of Thin Mints. I could feel Clementine's eyes on me, so I looked away. She had a row of file folders in a metal holder. Each folder was neatly labeled: Cookie Sales, Competition, New Customers, Old Customers.

"Is this your file for Girl Scout cookies?" I asked. "I hear you're pretty ruthless."

"Who told you that?" Clementine wondered, eyes narrowed.

"Gabby," I said. "The artist who's using them for some sculpture."

"How do you know her?" asked Clementine.

"I ran into her on the street the other day. She had so many cookies with her, I was curious."

Clementine nodded. "She's my dad's old friend, and she's been my best customer this month. I'm hoping she does a whole series of Girl Scout sculptures. I keep asking her to."

"Do you keep track of who gets what?" I asked.

"Sure," said Clementine, pushing her glasses farther up on her nose. "I keep records of every single sale, and I even created a computer program so I know how many boxes each person ordered last year. That'll help a lot for this season, which is just around the corner."

"And once the boxes go out, is there any way to track them?"

"What do you mean?" she asked.

"Like, each individual box. Say I had one and wanted to trace its origin. Would I be able to do that some way?"

"That would be impossible," said Clementine. "There are too many to keep track of. My sales volume is humongous—I'm the top seller for the entire state of New York. Third on the East Coast."

"That's amazing," I said.

"I know. I'm going for the world record."

"There's a world record for Girl Scout cookie sales?" I asked.

"Of course," said Clementine. "The record holder has sold a hundred thousand boxes. They call her the Cookie Queen. Except it's not fair, because back then there wasn't a bakery on every corner. Also, she started when she was six, and I didn't get to start until I was seven, but I'm doing my best to make up for lost time."

"How so?" I asked.

Clementine shrugged and inched closer to her desk

to stare at her files. "I can't tell you. Some things have to be kept secret."

Suddenly something small and furry appeared from nowhere and rubbed up against my leg.

"Ach!" I yelled. Looking closer, I was relieved to discover it was a cat. "Who's this?" I asked. The cat arched her back and purred as I stroked her chocolate-brown fur. When I stopped she blinked up at me with green eyes, as if begging for more.

"Thin Mint," Clementine said, like that was the most obvious thing in the world. "I named her that because of her coloring. Like the cookie."

"Oh, yeah," I said.

"Are you done with your questions? Because I have stuff to do."

"I do have one more," I said, stalling for time and trying to figure out why Clementine was acting so cagey. "What did you think of Sonya's Sweets?"

"What's that?" asked Clementine.

"It's the new soda fountain on Seventh Avenue. My friend's family opened it up a couple weeks ago."

"Never heard of it," Clementine said, glancing down at her feet.

Alarm bells went off in my head. I tried not to smile, but couldn't help myself. "Funny you should say that," I told her, "because I was looking through pictures of the grand opening just an hour ago, and I saw you in one of them. You were with an older woman. Maybe your mom?"

Clementine shook her head. She seemed nervous, which would make sense if she was lying. "My mom is in London for work."

"When did she go?" I asked.

"Last week," said Clementine. "I mean, a few weeks ago; I don't remember the exact date. And I've never even heard of Sonya's Sweets."

I stared at Clementine, trying to figure out whether she was bluffing. Her expression didn't tell me a thing. I guess I could've insisted I had photographic proof, but I didn't want to confront her like that. I was more interested in why she might be lying to me.

"Why are you asking all of these questions?" she asked.

"It's a long story," I said. "But you must've seen the place, since it's so close to here. It's right on the corner of Seventh Avenue and President Street."

"Sorry. I've never noticed," said Clementine. "But if you're done with your questions, you should probably go. I have a lot to do."

As she led me to the door, her dad, Rex, walked in. "Hi again, Maggie. Going so soon?"

"Yup," I said. "I'm on my way up to see Beckett now."

"So nice of you to drop by," he said, beaming. "Wasn't that nice, Clementine?"

Clementine shrugged.

Her dad handed her a large, colorful bouquet of flowers. "Here you go, sweetheart. And I got ice cream, too. Cookies and cream—your favorite."

Just then Thin Mint made a dash for the back of the room, followed by another cat, this one black and white.

"Oh, you have two cats?" I asked.

"Yup," said Clementine's dad. "Thin Mint and Samoa. We found them in the alleyway between this building and the one next door when they were kittens. Someone must've left them there."

"Samoa?" I asked.

"It's another type of Girl Scout cookie," Rex explained.

"Of course," I said, trying to keep the grin off my face. Because Samoa wasn't just the name of Clementine's kitty or a cookie—it was an important clue. Samoa was the person who signed for the shipment of chocolate that was supposed to go to Sonya's Sweets. Could Clementine be behind that, too?

Rex said, "We're a little obsessed with Girl Scout cookies in this household, as you can tell."

"Where'd they both go?" I asked, since both cats had disappeared, seemingly into thin air.

"Oh, they like to travel in the space between the walls of the building," Rex explained. "They're both skinny enough to fit through the cracks. I keep meaning to patch up the holes, but at the same time, I think it's nice that they have all the extra space."

"Huh," I said.

Suddenly something dawned on me. That scratching at the walls I thought I heard when I was babysitting last weekend? It must've been Thin Mint and Samoa scampering about. And that must be what makes Nofarm act so crazy in the building. Perhaps the kitties' antics behind the walls also fueled the rumors about the building being haunted.

At least that explained the ghost of Margaret. One mystery down, one to go!

I thanked Rex and Clementine for their time and said good night.

Before I went to Beckett's apartment I sat down on the steps in between floors and pulled out my notebook, because sometimes writing things down makes me think more clearly.

1) The ghost of Margaret is possibly a couple of cats named Samoa and Thin Mint.
2) Those cats are also clues to the soda fountain sabotage: The note at Ricki's store was written on the back of a box

of Thin Mints. The missing shipment of chocolate was signed for by Samoa.

3) Clementine would do anything to sell more Girl Scout cookies, but does that include sabotaging the competition? Possibly, but how am I supposed to prove it?

# Chapter 16

• • •

When I got upstairs, Finn and Beckett were on the floor building something with LEGOs.

"Welcome," Lisa said as she let me inside. "Thanks for coming tonight. And thank you for bringing your amazing brother."

"Amazing?" I asked.

"See, Mags—some people appreciate me," Finn called from the floor.

"Beckett is thrilled," said Lisa. "You two look so much alike."

"Thanks," I said. "If that's a compliment. I never know what to say when people tell me that."

"Say, 'yeah, I know,'" Finn said. "And it's definitely a compliment, because I'm exceptionally good-looking."

"'Exceptionally'?" I asked, raising my eyebrows and turning to Lisa. "See what I have to deal with?"

She laughed. "I've got a brother, too. So believe me, I know!"

"We won't be out as late this time," Caroline promised as she rushed out of her bedroom in a small, silver sequined dress. "Hi, Maggie. Good to see you."

She stepped into a pair of shiny black boots that were perched by the door.

"Stay out as long as you'd like!" Finn called from the floor. "We're good here, right, little man?" he asked Beckett and held out his hand.

Beckett slapped him five and giggled. "Bye, moms."

"Bedtime is at seven," said Caroline, glancing at her watch. "That's in twenty minutes. Okay, sweat pea? Hear me, Beckett?"

Beckett didn't answer until Finn whispered something in his ear. Then he giggled some more and said, "Okay, Mom. Don't worry. Have fun."

I could not believe how buddy-buddy these two were, when they'd met only ten minutes ago. Or how okay Beckett was with his moms leaving this time.

"Don't even ask," said Lisa, as if she could read my mind. "The two of them simply clicked from the moment they laid eyes on each other. So let's just go with it."

Once Lisa and Caroline were gone, I walked over to Beckett and Finn. "You guys need help?" I asked.

"No," said Beckett, encircling the LEGO city with his arms. "This is just for me and Finn to play with."

"Okay, no problem. I'll be right here if you need me." I flopped down on the couch. Then I opened up my backpack and pulled out the gigantic biography I'd just found at the library: *Jonas Adams, Brooklyn's King of Chocolate.* I still had to write my extra-credit report, and I didn't yet have enough material.

It seemed eerie but appropriate, writing about the Adams family in the actual Adams mansion. And with Finn to keep me company, the apartment seemed way less creepy.

In the first chapter of the book I learned that Jonas's father was a candy maker, too, except he wasn't so successful. His company went bankrupt when Jonas was just a young boy. He moved out when Jonas was twelve years old, but he left behind his tools. That's why Jonas started creating chocolate concoctions of his own. He and his mom made candy in their kitchen, and then Jonas traveled all over New York, selling individual pieces to pharmacies and five-and-dimes. Back then this was something that could be accomplished only in cold weather. New York summers were too hot and humid, and refrigeration and insulation technology was not so advanced. Whenever Jonas tried to sell chocolate door-to-door in the summer, his inventory melted.

This was interesting stuff, but it wasn't anything I could use for my report, so I wrote down a few notes and skipped ahead to when Jonas made his fortune. Just as Milo had told me, his mansion had the first passenger elevator in a private home in all of Brooklyn. Jonas lived there—here, I suppose—with his wife and his daughter. I couldn't imagine three people living in this gigantic, five-story mansion. What did they do with all the space? I suppose it didn't matter for my purposes. I searched for information about Margaret and finally saw her name buried deep in the chapter on domestic life near the end of the book.

*Like the other wealthy families in Brooklyn in the 1920s, the Adams family had a large staff. One summer, when they left for their vacation home in Maine, their elevator malfunctioned, and a nineteen-year-old Irish immigrant named Margaret O'Mally got stuck inside. Sadly, she perished.*

I stared at the few sentences about Margaret, hardly believing how little space was devoted to her despite her losing her life. "Sadly, she perished," the book said. End of story. End of *her* story, that is.

Suddenly I felt a chill, as if the cool night air had penetrated through the walls. The windows were closed, but they were old and drafty. I was shivering.

Then I heard something scratching in the walls.

Nofarm did, too, and raced to the back of the apartment. He barked and tried to paw his way through the wall.

"It's okay," I said to Nofarm. "It's just Thin Mint and Samoa, the cats that live downstairs." I knocked on the wall. "Time to go home now, guys."

"Who are you talking to?" asked Finn.

"There are a couple of cats that like to hang out on the other side of this wall," I said.

"Of course there are," said Finn, turning back to the LEGOs.

"Make this one bigger," said Beckett, pointing to the smallest tower.

"Whatever you say, boss," Finn replied. "This is awesome, by the way. I don't know why I ever gave this up."

Beckett's eyes got wide. "You mean you used to play with LEGOs, too?"

"Of course, dude. LEGOs are the best!"

I glanced at my watch. "Hey, Beckett. It's time to brush your teeth, okay, buddy? Then you've got to go to bed."

Beckett stood up and stomped his foot. "But I don't want to," he whined.

"Of course you do, dude," said Finn. "If you don't brush your teeth every night and every morning, they're gonna get all green and rotten and fall out, and then you won't be able to chew and you'll talk like this." Finn stretched his lips over his teeth and made his voice all low and scratchy, like an old man's. "I have no teeth. Will you hang out with me still?"

Beckett giggled.

"It's not so bad," Finn went on, standing up and hobbling across the room, hunched over and leaning on a pretend cane. "I get to have soup at every meal."

"I hate soup!" Beckett yelled, jumping up and running into his bathroom.

"Nice work!" I said to my brother as we high-fived.

"What can I say? I'm a natural," he said.

"Ha! I'd say don't let it go to your head, but I know I'm too late."

Finn shrugged, not able to deny a thing.

After we helped Beckett change into his red-and-blue-striped flannel pajamas, we each read him a story. Finn was totally excited to revisit *Where the Wild Things Are* after so many years. And I chose a new book called *B is for Brooklyn.*

"Good night, Beckett," I said.

" 'Night, dude," said my brother, tucking Beckett in and leaning in to give him a quick hug.

"Will you leave the closet door open?" asked Beckett.

"Sure," I said. "Think Margaret will come visit you tonight?"

"Probably," said Beckett.

"Who's Margaret?" asked Finn.

"She's my friend," said Beckett.

Finn looked at me, confused.

"I'll explain about Margaret later," I whispered as I propped Beckett's closet door open with one blue sneaker.

As Finn and I went back to the living room, I explained, "He's friends with the ghost, apparently." I was feeling pretty flippant about the whole thing. Now that I knew about the cats roaming around inside the walls, the whole thing seemed comical. That's why I laughed. And Finn did, too.

At least until we heard the eerie voice of an old woman.

Both of us went silent.

My ears perked up. Finn's did, too.

We looked at each other with raised eyebrows.

My first thought was, I must be hearing something, like maybe the neighbor's television or someone from outside. Except the voice was definitely coming from Beckett's room. And Beckett doesn't have a TV in his room.

"What's that?" asked Finn.

"Don't know," I said, watching the little hairs on my arms stand on end.

"Someone's singing, but I can't make out the song," Finn said, his eyes narrowed in concentration.

I looked toward Beckett's room, confused and, okay, I'll admit it, completely freaked out. Then it dawned on me. "It's 'Twinkle, Twinkle Little Star,' " I said.

"Why would we be hearing that song from Beckett's room?" asked Finn.

"I don't know," I said. "But we need to go in."

Finn gulped and stood up. Then we grabbed hands and walked to the bedroom. As we slowly opened the door, we found ourselves face-to-face with the ghost of Margaret.

# Chapter 17

◆ ◆ ◆

"AAAHH!!"

We screamed and hightailed it out of Beckett's room faster than you can say "There's no such thing as ghosts."

Standing in the living room, panting and looking at Finn, I realized something. We'd just broken the cardinal rule of babysitting: keep the baby safe.

Surely that could also be interpreted to mean *do not leave the baby with a ghost.*

Even if said baby claims to be friends with the ghost.

"We've got to go back in there," I told Finn.

He widened his eyes. "You're joking, right?" Then he took a deep breath and reconsidered. "No, you're right. Of course we need to go back. Come on."

We hurried back to Beckett's room and opened the door. The ghost was gone, and Beckett was sitting up in his bed, not scared or alarmed in any way. He just looked confused.

"Why'd you guys scream?" he asked, blinking at us calmly.

I checked in the closet and behind the drapes and under the bed. Then I looked out the window. The curtains in the window in the building across the street were wavering in the breeze, but otherwise all was still and silent.

"She's gone," I said.

"You guys scared her," said Beckett.

"We scared the ghost?" I asked.

"She's not a ghost," Beckett insisted. "She's Margaret."

I looked at Finn, who looked back at me.

Neither of us knew what to do.

Beckett yawned.

"Um, do you want to go to sleep?" I asked.

"Yes," said Beckett.

"Do you think Margaret will be back?" I asked.

"No. She's going to sleep, too," said Beckett.

"Has she ever bothered you or hurt you?" Finn asked.

Beckett looked at Finn as if he were a crazy person. "Of course not," he said. "She's my friend."

Finn looked at me and shrugged. Then we searched the room again, even though Beckett insisted his friend had gone home.

Apparently he was right. Finding nothing, I said, "Okay, good night, buddy."

"Good night," said Beckett before collapsing back on his bed.

Finn and I stayed in his room for a minute, unsure of what to do.

"You can go now," said Beckett.

"You're sure about that?" I asked.

"Yes," Beckett said. His voice had an edge to it, as though the little guy was losing patience with us. "I'm fine."

Back in the living room, Finn and I sat down on the couch, both of us staring at Beckett's door in silence.

"That was nuts," said Finn.

I had to agree. "Totally insane."

"And we both saw the same thing?" asked Finn. "Pale, scary figure with no legs?"

"Yup," I said. "That about covers it."

"Should we call the police?"

"And tell them what? We saw a ghost in this three-year-old's room, and we were the only ones who were scared? The kid is unharmed, and now the ghost is gone?"

"Okay, maybe that's a bad idea," said Finn. "But what are we supposed to do?"

"We'll just tell Caroline and Lisa," I said.

"Tell us what?" Lisa asked as she walked through

the front door and made us both jump. Doubly scared, the two of us yelled and grabbed hold of one another.

Caroline and Lisa stared at us, and then at each other.

"Rough night?" Caroline asked.

"We saw a ghost," Finn cried.

I giggled out of nervousness.

Caroline and Lisa looked as though they couldn't figure out the punch line to our joke. And I so, so, *so* wished that were the case—that we were joking. But we weren't, and we had to come clean.

"You know this Margaret that Beckett keeps talking about?" I asked.

"His imaginary friend," said Caroline. "Sure, we've discussed her with you before."

"Yeah, except she's not imaginary," I said, looking to Finn for confirmation. He nodded. "We know, because we saw her just a little while ago."

"In Beckett's room," Finn added.

"I thought it was the cat at first, but then I saw her. Margaret. The ghost of Margaret, I mean."

Lisa and Caroline ran to Beckett's room and we followed, all of us bursting through the door at once to reveal Beckett all alone and fast asleep.

Caroline checked in his closet and under his bed and even behind the dresser while Finn and I stood there, embarrassed.

"I know we sound crazy," I whispered as we all made our way back into the living room. "But we were eyewitnesses."

"Maybe you two should go home now," Caroline suggested gently as she squeezed my shoulder. "Get some rest."

Lisa handed us some folded bills and sent us on our way.

"Think they're going to ask us to babysit again?" asked Finn moments later as we walked home in the dark.

"I would say there's about zero chance of that," I said.

Finn shrugged. "Oh, well. It was fun while it lasted."

"It's too bad, because Beckett is crazy about you," I said.

"Yeah, I like him, too," said Finn. "He's got some awesome energy for a three-year-old. And he's a very cute kid."

"A cute kid who conjures ghosts," I said.

"Right," said Finn. "That's about the only downside of the night."

"I'm so going to have nightmares tonight," I said.

"You're lucky," Finn replied, thrusting his hands into the pockets of his hoodie. " 'Cause I'm not going to sleep at all."

# Chapter 18

• • •

Some kids—like my brother—don't like spending the night in new places, but I can't think of anything more exciting.

I love everything about sleepover parties. The mid-night movies with popcorn and other junk food; the silliness and late-night high jinks; the going to sleep surrounded by your closest friends, all wearing their cutest pajamas, knowing you're going to wake up in the morning right next to them.

Tonight was Beatrix's first sleepover party—and it was her birthday, too, so that meant we were going to have all sorts of fun. More important, I still hadn't come up with a logical explanation for the ghost in Beckett's room, so I definitely needed a distraction. Even if that distraction happened to be taking place directly next door to the supposedly haunted mansion. I tried not to think about that, but couldn't help but tense up when I walked past the old Adams place.

Okay, I lied.

I didn't just *walk* by the Adams mansion. I *ran*.

"Hey, you're the first one here," said Beatrix, opening the door to her apartment and giving me a quick hug.

"Happy birthday!" I said as I handed her a present wrapped in red paper with blue twine. "I'm not going to tell you what it is," I joked.

"Let me guess," she said, putting the book-shaped package next to her ear and giving it a shake. "Is it an airplane? No, wait a minute. I think it's a chocolate-covered banana."

"Oh, I can't believe you guessed," I said as we both laughed. I'd actually gotten her the first two books in a new gothic horror series. Not my thing—especially these days—but Beatrix likes scary stuff, and this was supposed to be good. At least that's what the lady who works at Community Bookstore down the street told me, and she's usually right.

We headed to Beatrix's room and she showed me her new iPad, a gift from her dad.

"Fancy," I said.

"I know," Beatrix agreed. "Ever since the divorce, his presents have been way over the top. Not that I'm complaining. It's all the guilt, my mom tells me."

We played a few rounds of Angry Birds before the doorbell rang again. This time it was Lulu and Sonya. They'd arrived together.

Sonya handed Beatrix a big bakery-style box as soon as she walked through the front door.

"What's this?" asked Beatrix.

"My famous chocolate-chip-peanut-butter cookies," she said. "Joshua's famous, I mean. He just taught me how to make them."

"Oh, are these from your new bakery?" asked Beatrix.

"It's a soda fountain, not a bakery," said Sonya, frowning slightly.

"What's the difference?" asked Beatrix.

Sonya's eyes widened. "Are you serious?" she asked. "There are a gazillion differences, which you'd know if you bothered to visit. But since you haven't, I figured I had to bring some cookies to you."

"Does this mean you tracked down the chocolate chips?" I asked.

"I didn't, but Joshua did," said Sonya. "Turns out they were delivered to the wrong address. Rather than going to one-eighty-seven Seventh Avenue, they were sent to one-seventy-eight Eighth Avenue."

"That's right next door to my building," said Beatrix.

"I know. It's the Adams mansion," I said.

"Right," Sonya agreed. "And the crazy thing is, Joshua found the entire case of chocolate chips in the alleyway between this building and the Adams mansion. Not like they got lost; it was more like someone was trying to get rid of them."

"Weird," said Beatrix.

"Totally," said Sonya. She patted the box in Beatrix's arms. "There's enough for everyone, if you want to open it now."

"I'm not really hungry," said Beatrix, setting the cookies down on the front table. "Let's save them for after dinner."

Sonya shrugged. I could tell she was hurt but trying to hide it. "Whatever you say."

Lulu handed Beatrix a gift bag stuffed with pink and green tissue paper. "Thank you," said Beatrix.

"Wait until you see what's inside," said Lulu. "Then you'll really thank me, because I made them myself."

"Cool!" said Beatrix.

"It's a pair of mittens with a matching hat," said Lulu, too excited to contain herself. "Whoops. Guess I spoiled the surprise."

"That's okay." Beatrix laughed. "I still don't know what color they are."

"Purple and red," said Lulu, before covering her

mouth with both hands. "Ah, I can't believe I did it again!"

We all laughed, and then Beatrix's mother came into the entryway.

"Oh, I'm so glad everyone is here," she said.

"Hi, Mrs. Williams," I said.

"Hi, Maggie, girls. Please call me Jessica. And please come to the dining room, because dinner is served."

We followed Beatrix's mom into the next room and sat down to a surprisingly delicious dinner of vegetable stir-fry with tofu.

"So, Maggie. Tell us about the ghost," said Lulu.

"Ghost?" asked Beatrix, raising her eyebrows.

"Yup. Maggie and Finn babysat at the haunted mansion last night," said Lulu. "And they saw the ghost of Margaret."

"No!" said Beatrix.

"'No' is right," I said. "We saw something that *looked* like a ghost, and, yes, it was scary at the time; but the more I think about it, the more I realize it couldn't have been a ghost."

"I don't know," said Beatrix. "There are some weird things happening at that place. I heard the lady in the top-floor apartment died a few months ago."

"Seriously?" I asked. "How old was she?"

"Like, ninety or something," said Beatrix.

"That's ancient," said Lulu. "She probably died of natural causes."

"Perhaps," said Beatrix. "Or maybe the ghost of Margaret scared her to death! I heard they didn't find her body for weeks. She's probably haunting the place now, too."

Beatrix was just kidding around, but after the weirdness of last night, I wasn't in the mood.

"Stop," I said. "One ghost is plenty for me to worry about, and I don't even believe in ghosts."

"Not even after you saw one?" asked Lulu.

"I don't know what I saw," I said, glad to see Beatrix's mom coming into the room with a large bowl of strawberries so we could change the subject.

"Dessert is ready," she said. "Now, who wants to sing 'Happy Birthday'?"

"That's so not necessary, mom," said Beatrix, cringing with embarrassment.

"Of course it is," said Lulu.

We sang "Happy Birthday" to Beatrix, and she blew out the candle lodged in the largest, plumpest berry with a single quick breath.

"No birthday cake?" asked Lulu.

"I don't like cake," said Beatrix, crinkling her nose.

"Since when?" asked Sonya.

"I don't know. Since always," Beatrix said defensively. "It's no big deal."

"You're right," Sonya agreed. "We can just open up the cookies I brought."

"You brought cookies?" asked Beatrix's mom. "That's so sweet." She turned to Beatrix. "You didn't tell me."

"Why is everyone making such a big deal out of the cookies?" Beatrix grumbled.

"They're by the front door," said Lulu.

"I'll get them." Beatrix's mom hurried out of the room, returning a few minutes later with a plate of cookies stacked neatly in a beautifully sweet, buttery pyramid.

I grabbed one right away, and so did Lulu and Sonya.

Beatrix took one reluctantly and put it on her plate.

"I'm not super hungry," said Beatrix, squirming in her seat and tucking her hair behind her ears. "Mind if I save mine for later?"

"It's your birthday," said Sonya. "Do whatever you want." She smiled, but we could all tell her feelings were hurt by the tone of her voice.

We ate our cookies in an awkward silence, all of us wondering why things had gotten so weird. At least, *I* wondered. As soon as I finished my last bite, Beatrix pushed her chair away from the table and said, "Let's pick out a movie for later tonight."

We followed her into the living room and she turned on the TV, heading straight to the horror-movie category on cable. "There's this new movie I want to see about someone who gets trapped in an insane asylum."

"Great!" said Lulu.

"Sounds perfect," Sonya agreed.

To be honest, I wasn't in the mood for a scary movie. I'd had another bad nightmare last night, this one starring the ghost of Margaret. She kept cleaning and cleaning my room, and I couldn't get her to stop even though I begged and pleaded. This doesn't sound like such a horrible scenario, I realize, but the Margaret in my dream was translucent and had hollow black spaces for eyes, and she sang this creepy version of "Twinkle Twinkle Little Star"; even just thinking about it later, in the company of my best friends, gave me the goose bumps. But I didn't want to argue—not when everyone else seemed so excited about the movie.

"Here it is," said Beatrix. "*Onslaught at the Asylum.*"

"Sounds pretty gory," Lulu said with a lot of enthusiasm.

Frozen on the screen was a gaunt and pale young

woman with a jagged scar across her face and blood dripping from her ears. Suddenly queasy, I looked away. "You guys want to watch this now?"

"No, let's set up our sleeping bags first," said Sonya. "That way I can hide at the scary parts."

"Brilliant plan," said Beatrix. "Let's put on pajamas, too. I'll go first."

Beatrix disappeared into her room, and the rest of us set up our sleeping bags on the floor of her den in a semicircle in front of the TV. I made sure to place my sleeping bag in between Beatrix's and Sonya's because I didn't want to be on the edge. Not that I had any reason to be scared, because I know there are no such things as ghosts, but still. I'd be lying if I said I wasn't completely freaked out being a mere twenty feet away from the Adams mansion—and having seen the "nonexistent" ghost.

When Beatrix came back she was wearing pajamas with purple polka dots and flowers. I went next, and changed into my new flannel pj's that had dogs all over them.

Lulu's pajamas were leggings and an oversize shirt with a giant owl and the words "Hoo's Sleepy?" on it. Sonya's pajamas were red-and-white striped and baggy.

"You look like a gigantic candy cane," I told her.

"I know. Isn't it great?" said Sonya, spinning around so we could see her from all angles. "They're new."

"Hey, before we watch the movie, let's play Would You Rather," said Beatrix.

"What's that?" I asked.

"It's this totally fun game I always play with my friends in the city," said Beatrix. "Basically, you get two options and you have to choose between them."

"I don't get it," said Lulu.

Sonya and I looked at Beatrix with puzzled expressions on our faces. "Neither do I," I said.

"Okay, then I'll go first," said Beatrix. "It's simple; one person poses an either-or question, and everybody else answers it. Like this: Would you rather kiss your boyfriend or Justin Bieber?"

"My boyfriend, for sure," said Lulu.

"That's sweet," said Beatrix.

"Me, too," I said, feeling a little weird because I wasn't exactly positive that I still had a boyfriend, it having been so long since Milo and I had spoken.

"Justin Bieber for me," said Sonya. "But that's easy, because I don't have a boyfriend. Yet. Although Joshua promised he'd share his gingerbread recipe with me. He makes the best."

"You think Joshua makes the best everything," I said.

"Yeah," said Sonya, "because he does. He must have some serious bakers in his family, because everything he's made for our store is amazing. He always says it's because it's a family recipe."

Lulu turned to Sonya and asked, "Would you rather eat rotten cheese or spend the night in a haunted mansion?"

"Definitely the cheese," said Sonya.

"But that could make you sick," Beatrix said.

"I know, but it would be over fast. You can swallow the cheese without even tasting it," Sonya reasoned.

"It depends on how big the cheese is," I pointed out.

"How big is the cheese?" Lulu asked Beatrix.

"It's a five-pound hunk," Beatrix said, holding her hands apart and frowning at the space between them as if she were actually holding some stinky cheese. "Definitely too big to gulp down."

"Having actually spent a lot of time in a haunted mansion," I said, "I'd take the cheese any day. Even if it's twenty pounds."

"Ugh, twenty pounds of cheese. It makes me sick just thinking about it," said Lulu. "How come there's no third option?"

"Because that's not how you play the game," said Beatrix.

"Okay, how about this one," said Sonya. "What's

scarier? Being trapped in a room filled with spiders or a room filled with snakes?"

"Snakes," said Lulu. "Because they can eat you alive."

"I think spiders are scarier," Beatrix said. "They're so small they can get anywhere. They can probably crawl through your ears and bite your brain."

"Yuck!" I yelled. "We need a new topic. What would you rather do: spend five minutes in the boys' bathroom or go to school with your underwear on the outside of your pants?"

"Underwear!" said Lulu. "As long as I could wear a long jacket so no one could see."

"That's cheating," said Beatrix. "You'd have to see them."

"Then I choose the boys' bathroom," said Lulu. "Then only half the kids at school would see me being mortified."

"Would you rather suffocate or drown?" asked Beatrix.

"Wow, that's heavy," said Sonya.

"Depressing, too," Lulu agreed. "I'd rather not die at all. How's that?"

Beatrix rolled her eyes. "We'd all rather not die, but the sad fact remains that we are going to. So if you had to choose, what would it be?"

"I want to die of natural causes in my sleep when I'm a hundred and five years old," said Lulu.

"That's not an option," said Beatrix.

"Fine," Lulu said. "I'd rather suffocate."

"Drown," said Sonya.

Beatrix said, "Me, too. I'd rather drown." She turned to me and asked, "What about you, Maggie?"

But I wasn't paying attention anymore. All I could think about was poor Margaret. Suffocating had to be a horrible way to go. How scary would it have been, being trapped in that elevator? I tried to picture the scene, but couldn't. I'd never even seen the elevator, since it had been boarded up for years.

Were the lights on or was it pitch-black?

Did Margaret know she was going to die, or did she think she'd be rescued?

How long had it taken, and what were her final thoughts?

Did she have any regrets? I mean, besides getting into the elevator to begin with.

She was only nineteen when she died. That's old compared to me, but young compared to how long most people live.

Margaret was still a teenager when her life ended. I'm twelve and a half now, which means in six and a half years I'll be nineteen. What if I had only six and a half years to live?

"Are you okay, Maggie?" asked Lulu gently.

"Fine," I said as I lay down with my head in my hands, staring at the ceiling.

Beatrix, Lulu, and Sonya went back to playing Would You Rather, but I'd had enough.

I flipped over onto my stomach, reached into my overnight bag, and pulled out my Dog-Walking Detective notebook. Then I flipped to an empty page and wrote:

> The box of chocolate chips was left in the alleyway between the Adams mansion and Beatrix's building—the same alleyway where Clementine found her kittens Samoa and Thin Mint.
>
> Coincidence or clue?

I stared at the words until my friends grew tired of their game and turned on the movie.

"You watching?" asked Lulu.

"Yeah," I said, closing my notebook.

I felt like I had to at least make an effort to watch with them. The problem was, from the very first scene the movie was all blood and guts and gore. Before we got too far into the story (if there *was* a story beyond all the scary stuff), I told my friends I was exhausted, climbed into my sleeping bag, and closed my eyes. And it turned out I wasn't faking, either—I fell asleep right away.

I don't know if they made it through the entire movie, or if they talked after, or played Would You Rather again, or what. All I know is, I was woken up in the middle of the night by a bloodcurdling scream.

I sat up with a start. Sweat poured down my forehead; my pajamas were soaked. And to my surprise, I realized the scream had come from my lips. My throat felt sore and everything.

But not only had I woken myself up, I'd also woken up Lulu, Sonya, and Beatrix. All of my friends stared at me, sleepy and alarmed.

"What's going on?" asked Beatrix, hopping out of her sleeping bag and pushing her hair out of her eyes to stare at me. "Are you okay?"

"Fine," I said. "I just had a nightmare."

"Some nightmare," Lulu said with a yawn. "I've never heard anyone scream like that."

"I know," said Sonya. "My heart is racing, like, a million miles a minute."

"Mine, too," I said. "Sorry."

"What happened?" asked Lulu.

"I have no idea," I said, rubbing my eyes. "I honestly can't remember."

Beatrix stood up and stretched. "I'm going to check on my mom, make sure she didn't hear."

"Was I that loud?" I asked.

Beatrix nodded.

I turned to Lulu and Sonya. "Really?"

They stared at me with sympathy, as if they wanted to say no but couldn't.

"Was it Margaret again?"

"I think so," I said.

"It's like she's haunting you from the grave," said Sonya.

"Let's not talk about graves," I said. "That totally creeps me out."

"Why?" teased Lulu. "I thought you didn't even believe in ghosts."

"I don't."

"I do," said Sonya. "I saw my great-grandmother once. Like, right after she died."

"You mean you saw her dead body?" asked Beatrix, coming back into the room and sitting down cross-legged on top of her sleeping bag.

"Did I wake your mom up?" I asked.

"Nope. She's snoring away."

"Good," I said.

"I saw her ghost," said Sonya.

"Whose ghost?" asked Beatrix.

"My great-grandma's, but you guys can't tell anyone."

"What do you mean, you saw a ghost?" I asked. Up

until now I'd honestly assumed Sonya was kidding around.

But her serious expression told me this was no joke. She sat up, crossed her legs, and told us the whole story. "So, my great-grandma was really old and living in Bangladesh; I hadn't seen her since I was a kid. And my mom was saying how we should really take a trip out there to visit with her before she died. I said, 'I really want to go see her, too. Before it's too late.' And my mom said, 'I'll make the phone call tomorrow and look into tickets.' "

We all nodded, totally entranced by the story.

Sonya took a deep breath before continuing. "And before I went to bed that night, I was brushing my teeth and saw this old woman in the mirror staring back at me. It was my great-grandma. I could tell because of her pink-and-gold sari. She waved to me and smiled, and then I blinked and she was gone, but I swear I saw her. I didn't really believe my eyes, though. So I went to sleep. But then the next morning I went downstairs, and my mom was sitting at the table with tears in her eyes. I asked what was wrong, and she said my great-grandma had died the night before."

I felt chills run up and down my spine.

"No way!" said Lulu.

Sonya's eyes were wide. "I'm dead serious. I started

crying. Things got way intense and emotional. My mom thought I was just sad because I'd never get to see my great-grandma again, but I was actually kind of freaked out. I told her why, and that's when my mom sat me down and told me that the same thing had happened to her."

"She saw your great-grandma in the mirror?" asked Beatrix.

"Nope." Sonya shook her head. "She saw her in the bedroom right before she was going to bed. She was wearing her famous pink-and-gold sari, and she waved to my mom and said, 'Good night.' But don't tell my mom I told you; she said we should keep it to ourselves because people wouldn't understand."

"I believe you," said Beatrix. "Because the same thing happened to me, kind of. What I mean is, sometimes I see my grandfather on the subway. And he died three years ago."

"Wait," I said, interrupting. "Don't you mean you *think* you see your grandfather, but really you see some old dude who looks like he did?"

Beatrix smiled at me. "I thought it was that at first, but I know it's his spirit because I can feel it. And also, on the day that he died, before I found out about it, even, I remember feeling this intense pain in my chest—like something was piercing my heart. And later I found out my grandfather had died of a heart attack."

"That's weird," I said. "But it doesn't sound like a ghost."

"I think we had this supernatural connection," said Beatrix. "Some of the people who have his spirit don't even look like him. Sometimes it's an old woman, and once it was a little boy, but I could see it in his eyes. My grandpa Mike."

I didn't know how to respond. I didn't want to talk about dead people anymore; the whole conversation left me feeling entirely unsettled.

"Hey, look," I said. "The sun is rising."

Everyone peered out the window. The sun crept up slowly, illuminating the quiet streets. The sidewalks were damp, which was funny because I hadn't even noticed it had been raining.

"Who wants to play Truth or Dare?" asked Beatrix.

"Me!" Sonya clapped. "I'll go first." She looked at Beatrix and asked, "Truth or Dare?"

"Truth," said Beatrix.

"Why haven't you been to Sonya's Sweets?" Sonya asked.

"That's not how you're supposed to play," said Beatrix, getting up and turning on the TV. "You're supposed to ask questions like, 'Have you ever kissed a boy?' or 'Have you ever cheated on a test?' "

"But we already know the answer to that," said Sonya. "You've kissed two boys."

"Okay, true. But you don't know whether I've ever cheated on a test," said Beatrix.

"Yeah—and I don't want to know that," said Sonya. "I want to know why you're avoiding my mom's new soda fountain. And why you didn't even try any of the cookies I brought over. We baked them especially for you."

"Ever since your mom opened up that store, it's all you can talk about," said Beatrix.

"Well, yeah," said Sonya. "That's because it's super exciting. And it's only been open for two weeks."

"Exactly," said Beatrix. "It's only been open for two weeks, and I've been busy. I'm totally planning on coming soon, but I haven't had the time."

"I'll bet another week will go by and you won't come," said Sonya. "And if you wait another week after that, we may not even be there. She's only going to give it a little more time before she shuts it down—unless Maggie can get to the bottom of things before then."

"No pressure," I joked.

"Oh, there's a ton of pressure," said Sonya.

"I was kidding," I said. "You know—sarcasm?"

"Right," said Sonya. "Of course. Sorry I missed that."

Beatrix sat back down on her sleeping bag and placed her pillow in her lap. "Okay, fine. I'll tell you why I haven't been to Sonya's Sweets and why I didn't get a birthday cake and why I can't have your cookies, but you have to promise not to tell anyone."

"Tell anyone what?" asked Sonya.

"Do you swear you won't tell?" asked Beatrix. "All of you?"

"Of course," Lulu agreed, as did the rest of us.

"What is it?" I asked, getting nervous.

"I'm borderline diabetic," said Beatrix. "That means I have to be super careful about what I eat, because if I'm not, I'll actually become diabetic, and that means taking lots of medication. And if anyone outside of this room finds out, I'm going to be furious."

"My grandma has diabetes," said Lulu. "What's the big deal?"

"The big deal is, it's a grandma disease," said Beatrix. "Except I have it, and there's no cure. I'm not supposed to have a lot of sweets. I always have to check my blood for my sugar levels, and if I go overboard, I could get really sick. That's what my doctor says, anyway."

"I'm so sorry," said Sonya. "I thought you were avoiding the shop because you didn't like me anymore."

"That's crazy! This has nothing to do with you. It's just hard, because I love all kinds of sweets, and I've never even had to think about what I ate before now. And I don't want to be surrounded by food I'm not allowed to have."

"Now I feel bad," said Sonya.

"Don't feel bad. You had no way of knowing," said Beatrix. "Let's just not talk about it anymore. Do you all promise not to say anything?"

"Of course," said Sonya. "And I'm so sorry if I was putting too much pressure on you. I had no idea."

"Don't worry about it," said Beatrix. "Just don't mention anything. Any of you."

"We won't," I said.

"Your secret is safe with me," Lulu promised.

"Good. Now let's keep playing," said Beatrix. "Who's going next?"

"Oh, I have a good one for Maggie," said Sonya, turning to me. "Truth or Dare?"

"Dare," I said.

"That's what I was hoping you'd pick! I dare you to go to the lobby of the building and sit there for thirty seconds," said Sonya, breaking out in a huge grin. "In your pajamas."

"No way!" I said.

"You have to," said Beatrix. "You chose a dare, and those are the rules."

"Fine, but thirty seconds is a long time," I said. "I'll only do it if you all come with me."

"But we're in pajamas, too," said Beatrix.

"Maybe we should change first," said Lulu.

I shook my head. "No way."

"Okay, but we're going to hide around the corner by the elevators. You've got to stand by the front door," said Sonya. "That's the deal."

"For thirty seconds," said Beatrix. "I've got a timer on my phone."

"If anyone from school sees me, I am never forgiving any of you!" I said.

"Why? You look cute!" said Beatrix, holding up her camera phone. "Smile!"

"Come on. No pictures!" I yelled, blocking the lens. "Now, let's get this over with." I tiptoed out of the den and opened the front door. We all crept out into the hallway, giggling nervously.

While we were waiting for the elevator, one of Beatrix's neighbors—some tall, skinny dude with a Yankees cap on his head and the *New York Times* tucked under one arm—came out and gave us the funniest look.

I tried to keep a straight face, but Lulu, Beatrix, and Sonya were cracking up, and eventually I did, too.

When the elevator doors parted, we all stepped in.

"Start the timer," I whispered.

"Not until you're in the lobby by the door," Beatrix replied.

"You're strict," I said. As soon as we made it to the ground floor, my friends pushed me toward the entrance to the lobby.

"I'm going!" I said, making my way there, relieved that so far, the coast was clear.

I felt so vulnerable. Sure, I was in my pajamas, but I felt kind of naked. I counted out the seconds. *One Mississippi, two Mississippi, three Mississippi . . .*

The first ten seconds seemed more like ten minutes.

Another five. And another. I could do this, I realized. I was almost done.

But just then I heard a noise coming from the front door. Someone was fumbling with his or her key. Please don't let it be someone from school, I thought as the door began to slowly creak open.

Beatrix's building has lots of apartments, and I could think of at least six kids from school who lived there, none of whom I wanted to see at the moment.

And it wasn't any one of them, but I felt no relief.

Because the person at the door? The one who waltzed right inside? Well, it wasn't a person at all.

It was the ghost of Margaret.

# Chapter 19

◆ ◆ ◆

I stood there completely frozen as she came in, a bag of groceries in one hand and a cane in the other. It was definitely her—the strange ghost who'd been in Beckett's bedroom the other night. When she looked up at me, I screamed as loud as I could and raced back to my friends, almost knocking Lulu over as I tried to hide behind her.

"Maggie, what's wrong?" asked Beatrix.

"You look like you've seen a ghost," said Sonya.

"And how come you're shaking?" Lulu asked.

From the concerned looks on my friends' faces, it was clear that I was the only one who saw the ghost of Margaret.

And as this fact hit me, I was left as confused as ever. Because the ghost was walking around like a real person, checking her mail and putting her keys in her purse before turning toward us.

"I did," I said, huddling closer to my friends. "See a ghost, I mean."

Beatrix glanced from Lulu to Sonya. "Um," she whispered. "There's no one here but Mrs. MacDonald, and she's alive."

"Oh," I said, and gulped. Because by now the "ghost" was right in front of us. And I had to admit, she looked surprisingly human. She was old, with short, curly gray hair and a pale face and small, round glasses. She wore a maroon pantsuit, the kind that might have been stylish fifty years ago.

"So you guys see her, too?" I whispered, just to confirm.

Beatrix nodded slightly as she cleared her throat and addressed the old woman. "Hi, Mrs. MacDonald."

"Hello, dear," said the ghost in a high-pitched, somewhat raspy voice. She pointed to the elevator. "Are you girls going up?"

"We are," said Beatrix, putting her hand on my back and pushing me forward a bit. "And my friend has a question for you."

The ghost looked to me, but I was too scared to speak. What was I supposed to ask, anyway?

"Go ahead," Lulu whispered.

But I couldn't find the words. I shook my head slightly, unable to take my eyes off the old woman.

"Okay, fine. I'll do it," Lulu said as she turned to Mrs. MacDonald, or the ghost, or whoever she was. "Is your first name Margaret?"

Mrs. MacDonald beamed at us. "It sure is. Do I know you girls from somewhere?"

Suddenly everything clicked into place.

Okay—not *everything,* but a few things.

"You were in Beckett's room last night!" I said.

She blinked at me from behind her glasses in silence.

I waited for her to argue with me, but she didn't.

"How did you get there? I know you didn't use the front door, because it was locked, and my brother and I were right there in the living room. We'd have noticed if someone came in."

Margaret tilted her head to one side and smiled at me. "I wasn't in Beckett's room," she said. "My reflection was."

"Huh?" I asked.

"My living-room window faces his bedroom window, and from his bed he sees my reflection in the mirror."

"He said you visit him at night," I argued, trying to sort this all out.

"And I do—or at least my image does. I go to my window every night, and if Beckett is there and if he's in the mood for a song, I sing to him."

I shook my head, trying to process this. Surprisingly, it made sense. Beckett's closet was lined with mirrors, and from the very first time I babysat he asked me to leave the closet door open—so he could get a better view of Margaret's reflection, although obviously I didn't realize it at the time. One thing still left me puzzled, however. "Why do you sing to him?" I asked.

Mrs. MacDonald smiled. "That's an excellent question, my dear. I suppose the simplest answer is, he asked me to. It happened for the first time last month, right when he moved in. He got very chatty and told me all about himself. His moms, the fact that they moved from just a few blocks away, his dog, Nofarm, and his old dog, Cookie."

"I know all about Cookie," I said.

"Anyway," said Margaret, "after chatting away, he suddenly asked me to sing him to sleep. So I did. And he must've enjoyed it, because he asked me the next night, too. It's become a funny little tradition, I suppose. Sweet little boy."

"He's great," I agreed. "You, um, surprised me and my brother the other night."

"You two surprised me, as well," Margaret said, smiling gently. "I didn't mean to scare you; I was just feeling shy. I'm surprised Beckett's parents didn't tell you about me."

"You know Caroline and Lisa?" I asked.

"Oh, no. I've never met them in person," she said. "But from the very first time I chatted with Beckett, I insisted that he tell his parents all about me. And he told me he did. I feel terrible for not going over there myself to explain and ask permission. But like I said, I'm shy. Plus, there are too many steps. I could never make it to the fifth floor on my own, now that the elevator is out of commission."

I shook my head, unable to keep from smiling at this news. "Beckett's moms think you're his imaginary friend."

"Oh, dear," said Margaret. "Please let them know that I'm real." Suddenly she gasped. "And I suppose you thought I was the ghost of Margaret—the one who's rumored to be haunting the Adams mansion."

I was almost too embarrassed to answer, but I managed a small nod.

"So, you know about Margaret the ghost?" asked Beatrix.

Margaret chuckled. "Of course I know about the rumors. I've lived here for a very long time. I even knew Jonas Adams when I was a little girl."

"You did?" asked Sonya, her eyes getting wide. "Did he give you free chocolate?"

Margaret chuckled. "Oh, he was very old by then,

and he'd retired. He got sick, too; had to spend a lot of time in bed. I know, because I was very good friends with his granddaughter, Trixie. I still am, in fact. But when we were girls, whenever we played at the mansion, we had to keep our voices down."

"Do you still speak to her?" I asked.

"Of course," said Margaret. "She lives a few blocks away."

"Is his whole family still in the neighborhood?"

"They sure are, but there aren't so many of them. Trixie had one daughter, and that daughter one son. He just started college this year. And all of them have stayed right here in Park Slope. Anyway, dear, I'm so sorry to have scared you. Please do explain the situation to Beckett's parents. I hope they don't mind."

"I'll let them know," I said as the elevator doors parted.

Margaret stepped inside.

"Are you girls coming?" she asked.

As we all filed into the elevator, Margaret surveyed us in our pajamas and smiled. "I never understood teenage fashion," she said.

My friends giggled.

And as the doors closed and the elevator ascended, I realized that Margaret seemed like a perfectly sweet old woman. How lucky Beckett was to have a friend next door, someone who was willing to give him a live concert every single night.

As I told myself all of this, I also reminded myself that there's no such thing as ghosts. The refrain was a familiar one—I'd been reminding myself of that fact ever since my fight with Milo.

And yet, the thing that struck me now was, I'd still been so scared when I thought I saw a ghost myself. I had to ask myself—*did* I believe in ghosts? Some of my closest friends did, and that news couldn't have surprised me more. Sonya and Beatrix were so sincere and so earnest in their beliefs about their grandparents wanting to reconnect with them, even from the grave. It gave me the chills.

"Where have you girls been?" asked Beatrix's mom as we all walked back into the apartment.

"We had to go to the lobby for something," said Beatrix.

"In your pajamas?" asked her mom.

"Yeah, it's kind of a long story," said Beatrix.

"Well, I'm making blueberry pancakes," she said. "So I hope you're all hungry."

"Starved!" said Beatrix. "But I'm going to get dressed before I eat."

"Me, too," I said. And after I threw on my jeans

and striped long-sleeve shirt, I went back to my notebook.

> The Adams mansion is not haunted. It's a creaky old building with uneven floors. The walls are a maze for two cats named Samoa and Thin Mint. And Margaret MacDonald, the neighbor, likes to sing Beckett to sleep.

As I studied my notes, I realized all of the explanations were perfectly reasonable. The Adams mansion is not haunted. It's just creepy, with some quirks and a lot of horrible history.

But as I told myself once again that there's no such thing as ghosts, I found that I didn't really believe it.

More important, though? I needed to talk to Milo. Immediately. Because suddenly something that hadn't made sense at all before, now did.

By the time I put my notebook away and packed up my sleeping bag and the rest of my things, my friends were at the dining room table eating pancakes.

I had a couple, too. Then I excused myself from the table and pulled my phone out of my coat pocket.

I sent Milo the following text:

> Sorry about before. My fault. I get that now. Can we talk?

I wasn't expecting a reply right away, but Milo texted me back immediately.

Sure. Want to come over?

There in twenty.

# Chapter 20

• • •

I hugged all of my friends good-bye and wished Beatrix a happy birthday.

"And thanks for inviting me," I said.

"Thanks for coming," said Beatrix. "I had a blast."

"Even though I woke everyone up with my blood-curdling scream?" I asked.

"Hmm," said Beatrix, narrowing her eyes, scratching her head, and pretending to think really, really hard. "You're right. That was ridiculous! Please never speak to me again."

We all cracked up, and then I thanked Beatrix's mom for everything and walked out the door.

Milo lives seventeen blocks away from Beatrix. Normally, it would feel like a super-long trek, and I'd take the bus. But this morning I decided to walk. I needed time to figure out what I was going to say to him.

I felt bad that it had been so long since we'd spoken, and confused and upset and annoyed that he'd been avoiding me. But after listening to Beatrix and Sonya last night, I was kind of starting to understand why he believed in ghosts—why it was so important to him, and why it was so insulting when I'd laughed at him for it.

But my inkling of understanding didn't mean I had a clue about what to say to Milo now. By the time I made it to his house I still hadn't figured it out, but I couldn't turn back. He was expecting me.

I ran my fingers through my hair, took a deep breath, and then rang the bell. Milo's grandma, Valerie, answered the door. Her dark hair was pulled into a loose French braid that hung down her back. She wore overalls and clogs and a navy blue bandana around her head. She seemed surprised to see me, but happy, too. "Good morning, Maggie," she said, smiling warmly.

"Morning. Is Milo home?" I asked. "I mean, I know he's home, because we just texted; I guess what I mean is—well, I don't know what I mean."

Valerie smiled and put her hand on my shoulder. "Please come in. I'm so glad you're here. Milo really needs to see his friends right now. I'll go get him."

But before she even called for him he appeared, running down the steps and pulling on his black puffy vest.

"Hey," he said, a slight smile on his face, as if this were just any old Sunday. "Want to go for a walk?"

"Um, sure," I replied.

"You two have fun," Valerie called, waving as we headed down the front steps of their house.

We walked for a while in silence. Not a hostile silence, though; it was more like neither of us knew what to say. But I decided to talk anyway. It only seemed fair, since I was the one who texted him this morning.

"So, I need to apologize," I began. "I shouldn't have laughed at you that day. About the whole haunted-mansion thing. I get that now."

I told Milo about all the crazy things that had happened at Beckett's house, from the crashing of Caroline's mirror to me and Finn seeing the "ghost" of Margaret in Beckett's room. Then I told him about meeting the real Margaret in Beatrix's building this morning. I laughed at the funny parts, but Milo didn't. He didn't really say anything as we walked, but I could tell he was paying close attention.

"So, even though there's no ghost of Margaret, it made me realize that ghosts do exist," I said. "It's because her memory haunts the place. She's a big presence in the building and I'm sure she always will be, and that got me thinking. I can see why someone would want to believe in a ghost. I mean, I can see why it would be comforting to stay connected to someone who's gone. Especially when you loved that person a lot, and especially when they died too soon. So I'm sorry. It was wrong of me to make fun of something you believe in, even if I didn't entirely understand it. And maybe I still don't."

I glanced at Milo out of the corner of my eye. His hands were jammed into the pockets of his vest, and he still wouldn't look at me.

"But you need to apologize to me, too," I said. "For avoiding me. That wasn't cool."

"I'm sorry," Milo said, kicking a rock. "You're right. I should've returned your texts and calls."

"It's not fair," I said. "All I wanted was to know what was going on with you."

Milo took a deep breath and puffed it out. "Okay, I'll tell you," he said. "Two weeks ago was the three-year anniversary of my mom's death."

"I'm so sorry," I said. "I mean, wow. I don't know what to say. That's intense."

"It was," he said. "It is, I mean. My grandma and I went to the cemetery to visit her grave, and then to the Donut Inn, which was her favorite diner. I ordered a Greek salad and a chocolate egg cream, even though I don't even like Greek salad, but that's what she always got. It's kind of dumb, I know."

I shook my head and linked my arm through his. "It's not dumb at all."

"Anyway, just eating her usual lunch made me feel closer to her. And I know that sounds kind of weird, but it's how I feel, and it's what we do. My grandma and I have been going there every year. Kind of in honor of her, I guess. Except this year something went wrong."

"Because of what I said?" I asked. "I'm so sorry for making fun. I really had no idea."

"No." Milo shook his head. "I mean there was something wrong with the salad. They didn't wash the lettuce or something, and I got food poisoning and was up all night puking in the bathroom. My grandma took me to the hospital the next day and everything."

"That's terrible!" I said.

"Yeah, it was a lousy few days. I was dehydrated and they had to give me an IV, and I hate needles. Then when I got home, I went to bed and kind of lost all track of time. My grandma told me I slept for three days straight, practically. And when I woke up and was finally feeling better . . . I don't know. I still felt lousy. Not ready for school, and mad at you. I mean, I'm not dumb—I know my mom isn't actually around all the time. She can't, like, see me or talk to me or anything. But when I'm near her grave, or eating her favorite food, or playing chess sometimes, it's like I can feel her presence around me."

"Like a ghost," I said.

"Yeah." Milo shrugged ever so slightly. "That's the best way to describe it, probably. I should've told you before. I mean, I don't care about the ghost of Margaret or some dumb haunted mansion. But what I was afraid to tell you the other day—what I want to tell you now—is that I *have* to believe in ghosts. Because if I don't, then I'm really all alone."

He finally looked me in the eye, and seeing the hurt look on his face almost broke my heart. "I'm sorry I stormed off that day. And I'm sorry I've been out of touch. I should've explained all this sooner, I guess."

"It's okay," I said. "I'm sorry, too. Let's just forget about it. Start over."

"Deal," he said.

"Good."

We kept walking.

"So, did you ever figure out who's been messing with Sonya's Sweets?" he asked.

"Not yet," I said. "But I think I'm close. There are two possibilities, actually—or maybe two people are working together, although I'm not sure how or why. But did you know that Jonas Adams has family who still live in the neighborhood? His great-grandson is in college, actually."

"You think his family could be behind the whole thing?" asked Milo.

"Maybe," I said. "And there's also this surly Girl Scout I know who's totally obsessed with Girl Scout cookie sales. She was at the opening; I know because I have a picture of her. And yet she keeps denying it. So I have this weird hunch."

"Huh," said Milo. "Your weird hunches usually turn into something."

"Yeah," I agreed, nodding. "And hopefully this one is no exception."

I told Milo I had to get home, take a shower, and go through my notes again.

We parted ways, and I was just a few blocks from my house when I nearly ran right into someone familiar. Two someones, that is: Joshua and Felicity from Sonya's Sweets, except they were nowhere near the soda fountain. They were standing on the corner. Oh, and they were kissing.

Yup. That's right. Kissing.

I stopped and started backing up, intent on going in another direction to avoid them, but then Joshua spotted me and broke away.

"Hey, Maggie!" he said. "Wait!"

I had no choice but to approach. Still, seeing Sonya's crush making out with Felicity, Sonya's cousin? It was the last thing I expected to see, and the last thing I *wanted* to see.

But suddenly something major clicked into place.

Sonya had been complaining about all of Felicity's late-night texting. The person she'd been texting with called himself JAM.

Joshua's last name was Marcus. Joshua Marcus. Could JAM be his initials? And if so, what did the *A* stand for?

I thought about the mini-chocolate-bar tattoo on Joshua's wrist. And how he was always talking about his family recipes. And how Jonas Adams, Brooklyn's King of Chocolate, had a great-grandson who'd just started college, and was still living in Park Slope.

Maybe Joshua's middle name was Adams, and he's Jonas Adams's great-grandson.

Could it be? There was only one way to find out.

"Hey, what's your middle name?" I asked Joshua.

He turned to me, surprised. "What do you mean?" he asked as a panicky expression flashed across his face.

"It's Adams, isn't it?" I asked.

"What are you talking about?" Felicity asked.

"He's JAM," I said, pointing to Joshua. "Joshua

Adams Marcus. That's what you call him when you text each other, right?"

"Yes, he's JAM," said Felicity. "But why do you care about his middle name?"

"Because I think he's named Adams after his great-grandfather," I said, definitely aware of the fact that Joshua hadn't yet denied this.

"Wait," said Felicity, turning to Joshua. "Who is your great-grandfather?"

Joshua turned bright red. "It's Jonas Adams, but please don't tell anyone. It's embarrassing."

"Tell anyone what?" asked Felicity.

"That my great-grandfather founded Adams Chocolate," said Joshua.

"Why would you hide something like that?" asked Felicity. "Adams Chocolate is delicious."

"I know," said Joshua. "But I never tell people that, because I want to succeed on my own, not because my great-grandfather created Adams Chocolate."

"I don't see how sabotaging Ricki's store is going to make you successful," I said.

"Um, what are you talking about?" asked Joshua.

"You're trying to eliminate the competition, right?" I asked. "That's why you broke the picture window, switched the salt and sugar, and made the chocolate chips disappear."

"Wait, I'm the one who *found* the chocolate chips," he said.

That's what you told people, I thought but didn't say. "Maybe you found them because you're the one who hid them," I said.

"But I already told you," said Felicity, "I'm the one who poured the salt into the sugar bowl."

"But Joshua told me he did it," I said. "And one of you has got to be lying, unless you're working together."

"No, I was lying," said Joshua, "because I didn't want to get Felicity in trouble. As for the picture window, I have no idea who broke it. But I promise you I'm doing everything I can to make sure Sonya's Sweets is a success. I feel lucky to have that job, and Ricki's doing incredible things with the store. I wouldn't do anything to harm anyone."

I studied Joshua. He seemed sincere. And something about his plea made me believe him.

"So you don't know anything about the picture window?" I asked.

"Sorry," said Joshua.

"You should go," Felicity said to him suddenly. "I need to talk to Maggie alone."

"Are we okay here?" Joshua asked me. "Do you believe me?"

I thought about this for a few moments. “I do,” I said.

“And you’ll keep my secret?” asked Joshua. “I promise you, I am not trying to mess with Ricki’s business.”

“Okay,” I said. “Sure.”

“Thank you.” He put his hands together and bowed a small bow. Then he turned to Felicity. “Text me later,” he said.

“Of course, Jammy,” said Felicity. She waved goodbye, and as soon as Joshua was out of sight she pulled me to the curb and sat me down.

“Okay, Maggie. What you saw? You’ve got to promise me you won’t tell anyone.”

“I can’t believe you’d do this to your own cousin.”

“Look, I can explain. I’ve been hiding this to spare Sonya. I know she has an enormous crush on Joshua, and that’s exactly why I insisted we keep our relationship a secret. I didn’t want her to get hurt, but the fact remains that I like him, too. And he’s actually my age. It’s, like, okay for us to be together. I’m not doing anything wrong.”

The way Felicity said this made it seem as though she wanted me to say that everything she did was okay. And some of it was okay: if she liked Joshua and Joshua liked her, then of course they could be together. They were both adults, or almost adults—more adult than me and my friends, anyway. But sneaking around and lying to her cousin? And then asking me to lie about what I saw? That was wrong, and there was no way I was going to let her get away with it.

"You can tell Sonya whatever you want. Or don't tell her anything, but I can't keep this a secret. She's one of my best friends."

"Exactly," said Felicity. "I love her, too. That's why I think she should be spared the pain."

I shook my head. "No. It's not fair."

Felicity hid her head in her hands. "This is a disaster. I never should've come to New York. I knew I'd mess things up. Ricki and Sonya have been so nice to me, welcoming me into their home and giving me a job, and I've been terrible to them."

"So it's you?" I asked.

"What do you mean?" asked Felicity.

"Are you the one trying to shut down Sonya's Sweets?"

Felicity looked at me and laughed. "No! Why would I do that? I love my aunt and my cousin. And I know I'm lucky to be here. It's just—I can't work at the soda fountain. I'm no good at it."

I couldn't exactly argue with Felicity. She was a horrible employee. "Are you sure you're not trying to ruin things there on purpose? Like, maybe you think if it had to close down, you wouldn't have to work there anymore?"

"What are you talking about?" asked Felicity.

"Well," I said, "you and Joshua were laughing right after the window got smashed. And you forgot to mail the electric bill. And, I don't know—you keep spilling stuff."

Felicity laughed again. "Believe it or not, Maggie, those are honest mistakes. I'm not guilty of sabotaging the store. I'm only guilty of vanity."

"Huh?" I asked.

"Hold on. I'll show you." Felicity opened up her purse, dug around in it for a few moments, and then pulled out a thick pair of glasses, which she put on her face.

"You wear glasses?" I asked.

Felicity nodded, blinking behind her thick lenses. The frames were dark purple and chunky. They were so ugly they were cool. Or at least they would be on someone else; on Felicity they just seemed wrong.

"Try to tell me I don't look hideous in these," she said. "My eyes are so weak I can't even wear contacts, so I'm supposed to have these on all the time."

I tried to look at Felicity objectively. She definitely looked different, but not hideous. Not that I should have to reassure her at the moment. And then my mind began to shift gears, as some things—but not everything—fell into place.

"It was you who mixed up the salt and sugar," I said. "Right? And Joshua lied for you because he likes you?"

"Yup." Felicity nodded. "He didn't want me to get into trouble. Ricki was already upset with me because I'd dropped an entire case of straws on the floor, which was still wet from when I tipped over the mop bucket earlier."

"That's sweet of him," I said.

"I know," said Felicity. "He's a sweet guy. And I know it was inappropriate to laugh right after everyone was freaking out about the baseball that broke the window, but I couldn't help myself. Joshua made this really funny joke and I lost it."

"Wait," I said. "What baseball?"

"The one that went through the window," Felicity said, as if it were obvious. "Hold on a second." She dug through her bag and pulled out a baseball, holding it up to me triumphantly.

I took the ball and turned it over in my hands. "Where did you get this?" I asked.

"I just told you," Felicity said impatiently. "I picked it up off the floor after it sailed through the window."

"So a baseball broke the window?" I asked.

"Yeah," she said. "Didn't you know that?"

"No one knew that," I said. "We've been trying to figure it out forever. This changes everything. This is important evidence."

"Really?" asked Felicity, tilting her head to one side and squinting. "I never thought of it that way."

"Then why have you been carrying it around for two weeks?" I asked.

She smiled and blushed and looked down at the sidewalk. "Joshua and I kissed for the first time on opening day, and I wanted to keep the baseball so I'd never forget about it."

"Isn't that kind of a strange souvenir?" I asked. "Why not keep your paper hat, for instance? Or maybe a spoon?"

"Huh," said Felicity. "I guess I could have, if I hadn't already lost my hat. But the thing is, you can't argue with matters of the heart, Maggie."

I let out a laugh. "What do you mean by that?"

"Oh, I don't know," she said, flipping her hair over her shoulder. "I heard it in a movie once, and I liked the way it sounded."

I had a bunch of questions I could've asked, but decided not to. Something told me that the normal rules of logic just didn't apply to Felicity. "Um, that's really sweet," I said, trying not to lose my patience. "But I think you probably should've told me about this. And your aunt Ricki, who's thinking about shutting down her store because of all of this unexplained stuff."

Felicity looked at me guiltily. "She does seem kind of stressed, I suppose. I probably should've asked her why. I guess I've been preoccupied."

"Obviously," I said as I stood up and backed away.

"Wait," said Felicity. "Can I get my ball back?"

"No, I need to figure out where this came from."

"But it's mine," she said. "And I'll tell you where it came from. One of the kids at the opening threw it."

"Who?" I asked.

Felicity cringed. "I can't tell you because he swore me to secrecy."

"But he committed a crime!" I said.

"It was an accident," said Felicity. "A simple mistake. The poor kid threw the ball to his friend, and didn't realize his friend wasn't paying attention."

This time it was my turn to laugh. "You mean the whole thing was an accident?"

Felicity nodded.

"Are you positive about that?" I asked.

She nodded again.

"You're not just making it up? I need to know. This is very important."

"I swear to you," said Felicity. "This kid came up to

me and asked for the ball back because he was worried about getting into trouble. And I promised him if I could keep it, I'd never tell."

"So he didn't have it out for the store or anything," I said. "The note had nothing to do with the shattered window?"

Felicity shook her head. "He loves Sonya's Sweets. He's been back almost every day since. He's addicted to Joshua's Key lime pie. I don't blame him; it's spectacular."

"Okay. Thanks for the information. Is there anything else you think I should know?" I asked.

"Nope," said Felicity. "I think that covers it. Um, you're not going to tell Sonya about me and Joshua, right?"

"Nope," I said, tossing the ball in the air and catching it again.

Felicity seemed relieved, but only until she heard my next words.

"I'm not going to tell her, because you're going to."

Felicity started to argue but then seemed to think better of it. "Do I get the baseball back, at least?"

I tossed it back to her, but she missed and it rolled off the sidewalk. Felicity started to dart after it, but I stopped her because a car was speeding down the street.

Once the coast was clear and we recovered the ball, Felicity thanked me. Then she took off her glasses, put them in her purse, and tripped over a gigantic crack in the sidewalk.

"Maybe you should wear them home," I suggested.

"Maybe I will," Felicity grumbled.

# Chapter 21

◆ ◆ ◆

Lulu called me later that night. "You left Beatrix's in such a hurry this morning. Is everything okay?"

"Everything is great," I said. "I talked to Milo and we're good—and I'm pretty close to figuring out who's been messing with Sonya's Sweets."

"Cool! Who is it?" she asked.

"Long story. And I don't want to name any names until I get hard evidence."

After I hung up, I wrote down some thoughts.

*Joshua is the great-grandson of Jonas Adams, Brooklyn's King of Chocolate. And yet, he is innocent.*

*The shattered picture window happened by accident.*

*Felicity is a huge klutz, and pretty absentminded, too. But she's not guilty, either.*

*So only one person could've written the note: Clementine.*

I slammed my notebook shut, realizing that all I had to do now was prove it.

After school the next day, I hurried to Beckett's apartment. I owed his dog a walk, and I owed his moms an explanation.

Luckily, Caroline was home. She and Beckett were baking cupcakes, both of them up to their elbows in flower and sugar.

"Hi, Maggie!" she said.

"Hi," I replied. "Guess what? I met the ghost of Margaret this weekend."

"Hmm?" asked Caroline, concerned and probably wondering whether it was time to relieve me of my dog-walking duties.

"Turns out, Beckett's imaginary friend is real!" I told her.

"Please don't talk about G-H-O-S-T-S in front of B-E-C-K-E-T-T."

"B-E-C-K-E-T-T spells Beckett!" Beckett told me proudly.

"Good job, sweetie," his mom said, kissing him on the top of his head.

I explained the whole story, without using the word "ghost." "So if you want me to babysit, just know I'm not crazy. My brother isn't, either. And since I already have a job walking dogs, maybe you should get in touch with him."

"Oh, Mommy, please can Finn babysit again?" asked Beckett.

"Sure," Caroline said. "Maybe this Saturday. I'll give him a call, okay?"

"Do we have to wait until Saturday?" asked Beckett. "That's so far away!"

I left Caroline and Beckett to figure things out and took Nofarm out for a quick spin around the block. After dropping him off back home, I went to apartment 4A and knocked three times.

Clementine answered the door and didn't seem exactly thrilled to see me. "What do you want now?" she asked.

"That's an excellent question," I said, walking into the apartment. "For one thing, I'd like to know why you want Sonya's Sweets to go out of business."

"What are you talking about?" asked Clementine.

"Don't deny it," I said. "I know you were behind the note. It was written on the back of one of your cookie boxes. And I know you signed for that delivery for Sonya's Sweets, too."

"What delivery?" she asked.

"The giant box of chocolate chips that you ditched in the alley next to your building—*Samoa*!"

Clementine put her hands on her hips and narrowed her eyes at me. "I have no idea what you're talking about."

I wondered how I was going to get her to admit the truth, and then I noticed something at her feet.

"What's in the box?" I asked, trying to keep the smile off my face.

"Girl Scout cookies," Clementine replied quickly.

*Too* quickly.

"That's funny," I said, bending down so I could get a closer look. "When I was a Girl Scout way back when, all of the cookie boxes had the official Girl Scout insignia on them. Yet this box is blank."

A guilty expression flashed across Clementine's face as she stepped in front of the box. "That must've been a really long time ago, because you're so old. Things have changed."

I quickly picked up the box, reading the label out loud.

"To: Sonya's Sweets," I said, smiling because I finally had the evidence I needed. "This is a box for Ricki's store."

"I told you, I don't know what you're talking about," said Clementine. "This box came to me. And I've never even heard of Sonya's Sweets. Or whatever you call that place."

"Oh, Clementine, give it up," I said. "I have a picture of you at the opening with your mom. Yes, you're wearing dark glasses, but I know it's you. You planted the note. And you stole the boxes. It's illegal to tamper with the mail. Did you know that? That's serious fraud. You can go to jail for it."

"I didn't steal the boxes," said Clementine. "The first one got delivered to my house accidentally; all I did was leave it in the alley. And this one just arrived. The mailman dropped it off. It's not my fault he's confused."

"And what about the note?" I asked.

"What note?" asked Clementine.

"The note written on the back of a box of Thin Mints in blue highlighter," I said. "Probably the same blue highlighter that's on your desk right now."

"I didn't break the window," said Clementine, her bottom lip quivering. "The note was stupid, a bad idea: But I didn't break the window, and I've been so scared I'd be blamed for it."

Real tears streamed down her face. "I never meant to hurt anyone," she yelled. "All I wanted to do was sell the most cookies in the world, and it's been so hard lately. First cupcakes came to town, and then ice cream and frozen yogurt. There's too much competition. How many sweets can one person buy?"

"You're worried about competition?" I asked. "That's why you're trying to shut down Sonya's Sweets?"

"Yes, of course. Are you going to call the police?" Clementine asked. "Please don't do that. I'm sorry. I'll never do anything like this again."

"Don't apologize to me," I said. "You need to talk to Ricki. Let's go. You can tell her everything, right now."

# Chapter 22

◆ ◆ ◆

Two weeks later, Milo and I headed over to Sonya's Sweets for a hot chocolate. We've been going almost every Friday after school. Joshua usually makes it for us, and he always adds extra marshmallows to my cup.

He's still working at the soda fountain, but Felicity is long gone. Gabby helped get her a job at a local gallery, a place for which she's much better suited. She still visits occasionally—you know, to see her boyfriend, Joshua. Or Jammy, as she likes to call him. Sonya isn't thrilled by this development, but she's gotten used to it. Kind of. She and Joshua are still buddies. He's teaching her all his family's baking secrets. Usually I see the two of them at work together, but today Joshua stood alone behind the counter.

"Hey, Jammy," I said. "Where's Sonya?"

"She's at home, working on the new picture

window," Joshua explained. "And you promised not to call me that, remember?"

"Sorry," I said with a grin. "I keep forgetting. That's great about the window, though."

"Yeah," said Joshua. "Her dad just got back from India, and they're designing one that's even bigger than before."

"Awesome," said Milo.

Joshua nodded. "Yup. And this time they're using shatterproof glass."

"Even though Maggie managed to get all those evil zombie Girl Scouts off the streets?" asked Milo.

I socked him in the shoulder. "Stop. Clementine isn't a zombie."

"She's just an evil Girl Scout?" asked Milo.

"Not evil. Just confused and conflicted. Poor kid."

"Hey, she got off easy," said Joshua as he sliced into a fresh, just-out-of-the-oven cherry pie. "I'd say she was lucky."

I had to agree. After I caught the guilty Girl Scout with the box from Sonya's Sweets, we marched to the soda fountain and she confessed to Ricki.

Ricki was so grateful to have answers that she decided not to press charges. Instead, she had a long talk with Clementine's dad, and the two of them agreed on a suitable punishment. Clementine would have to retire from the cookie business—the pressure to be the best was clearly too much for her to handle. Instead she was doing some volunteer work, baking cookies herself and donating them to bake sales all over Brooklyn.

And speaking of retiring, I don't need to. Retire from dog walking, that is.

Mr. Phelps loved my report, so I got my extra credit. My parents were not happy about my D+, but they agreed to put me on "double secret probation" and let me continue to walk dogs as long as this kind of thing never happened again. And it never will!

I drained my hot chocolate and popped a half-melted marshmallow into my mouth. "See you guys later," I said, sliding off my stool. "I've gotta get to work."

"Wait," said Milo. "I'm coming, too."

"Cool," I said. We waved to Joshua and headed up the street.

"Where to first?" asked Milo.

"Nofarm, of course," I said.

"You mean we're going to the haunted mansion?" Milo said, eyes wide and teeth chattering in mock fright.

"That's right," I said with a grin. "But don't make fun."

I'd already admitted to Milo that whenever I walked into the Adams mansion, I thought about Margaret. Not Beckett's buddy Margaret from across the street, but

Margaret O'Mally, the young Irish maid who died in the elevator. I guess you could say she haunts me, or at least her memory does, but that's okay. I'm ready to embrace it. Because the thing is, as Milo and my friends taught me, ghosts do exist.

They don't have to be the creepy monsters that cause nightmares or do harm. They can take the form of memories, of feelings, or of a hard-to-define presence. Or of something else that's impossible to explain, but that's totally okay—just because something can't be explained doesn't mean it doesn't exist.

Sometimes ghosts can feel as real as the taste of salty apple pie on your tongue, or the perfect bite of chocolate chip cookie. Some people want to be haunted by their memories, and that's fine. It's not for me to judge. I get it. And also? I believe.

Annabelle isn't monkeying around in her latest adventure. She and her friends are desperate to come up with enough cash to see their favorite bands this summer, and a regular old lemonade stand just won't cut it!

Read on for an excerpt from the latest book in the Annabelle Unleashed series.

## the big move

I woke up early on Saturday morning and panicked—big time!

The problem? I had no idea where I was. Sunlight streamed in through large, pretty but unfamiliar-looking picture windows. It made bright rectangles on the plush peach carpet below.

Peach carpet, I thought. My room doesn't have peach carpet. And it's not this big. Where am I and what am I doing in this place? Was I kidnapped by aliens in my sleep? Am I on a spaceship hurtling toward Mars? And if so, who knew spaceship bedrooms looked so much like human ones? And how come I don't feel as if I'm racing through the stratosphere? Have those aliens already messed with my brain? With their special alien brain scrambler?

I took a deep breath and tried not to panic.

Then I tried to figure out what a special alien brain scrambler would look like.

It would have a lot of wires and blinking lights, I decided as I rubbed my eyes. That's when I realized

I was under my favorite blanket. It's fuzzy, blue, and flannel with pink polka dots. My blanket happened to be on my trusty old bed, which is twin-size with a wooden headboard. The rest of my bedroom furniture was in this strange new place too: desk, bookshelf, and dresser all in a row on the opposite wall. Hmm. All my familiar stuff was there, except my bedroom wasn't what I was used to.

I was seriously confused. I mean, what was going on? This whole morning made no sense. Or, I should say, the whole kidnapped-by-aliens thing was the only explanation. Like, maybe they brought along all my furniture so I wouldn't realize right away that I'd been captured. And if so, the plan kind of worked. I'm probably halfway to Mars by now.

Except for the fact that aliens don't exist. And if they did, what would they want with me, Annabelle Stevens, a short and spunky sixth grader?

I gasped when the following thought occurred to me: maybe Mars needs a whole slew of short and spunky sixth graders. Maybe they wanted to clone me into an all-girl army to fight for peace and justice. Actually, that would be pretty cool. Except, what if they plan to use my clone army for evil purposes, like to conquer Earth? I'd become the face of evil for all humankind. That would be the worst!

It's a good thing human-cloning technology doesn't exist, as far as I know, and like I said before—neither do aliens. So what *was* going on? As the sleep fog from my brain cleared, I remembered what yesterday was: moving day!

Aha! Now wide awake, I sat up straight. Excitement gurgled in my belly because today was no ordinary day. Big things were happening, and none of them had anything to do with aliens.

Here's the thing: I'm living in a brand-new house and I just woke up in my brand-new bedroom.

Me, my mom, and my stepdad, Ted, plus my scruffy mutt, Pepper, all moved here less than twenty-four hours ago.

Oh, wait. Let me back up a minute and explain a few things. My name is Annabelle Stevens. I'm eleven years old—practically twelve. I am short and skinny with straight blond hair that's long and parted slightly to the left. It's all one length—I don't have bangs. My eyes are brown and my skin is so pale that it burns easily. That's why my mom makes me wear sunscreen every single day. And when we go to the beach, she insists that I wear a hat, even though hats look dorky on me. Plus, they always make my hair even flatter than usual.

I live in Westlake Village, which is outside of Los Angeles, which is in Southern California, which is in the state of California, which is in the United States of America, which is on the continent of North America, which is on the planet Earth, the third planet from the sun.

Our sun, anyway. There could be other solar

systems out there—no one knows for sure. But I guess I've gotten a bit off my subject.

It could be because geography has been on my mind a lot since our big move. Not that the move was so big. That's the funny part. When I left for school yesterday, I lived on Clemson Court. And when I came home from school, I lived on Oakdell Lane.

Today is Saturday and here I am: in a new house, on a new block, in a new neighborhood. We still live in the same town—Westlake. Also, my new house is merely one mile away from my old house. But it feels as if it's a whole world away because we live in an entirely different housing development. Our old neighborhood is called Morrison Woods. Our new neighborhood is called Canyon Ranch.

Another crazy thing about this new house is that my room is literally twice the size of my old room. That's why it felt so weird waking up there this morning. I'm not used to having so much space. Not that I'm complaining. Having a big room is great and the best part is that it's large enough for Rachel, Claire, Yumi, and Emma, my four best friends in the entire universe, to sleep over. And that's exactly what they're going to do tonight!

"Oh, good. You're up," said my mom, poking her head into my room. Her blond curls were piled up in a high ponytail and she was rubbing her belly. She's been doing that a lot lately, because she's pregnant.

Yeah—that's right. That's the other big news in my life. The main reason my family moved to this big new house is that my mom and Ted are going to have a new baby. More important, it means that in a few months I'm going to have a brother or sister. I am dying to know which, but my mom and Ted are insisting on keeping it a surprise.

I wish they'd change their minds and find out so they can tell me. I've even told them they can have the doctor call me and I'll keep it a secret from everyone, but they were not so into that idea. It's too bad, but regardless of whether they're having a boy or a girl I'm going to be a big sister, which is huge! I've been an only child for most of my life. Then last year my mom and Ted got married. Ted has a son named Jason, but he's super-old—twenty-one—and he's away at college. So even though I'm kind of a little sister now, I still feel pretty much like an only child. So it'll be weird to have a baby around—but hopefully weird in a good way.

In the meantime, my mom's belly is so big and round she looks as if she swallowed a regulation-size soccer ball.

"I would say I'm barely awake," I replied, yawning as I peeled off my covers and climbed out of bed. "When I opened my eyes this morning, I didn't know where I was."

My mom laughed. "That same exact thing

happened to me! I guess it'll take a bit of time to get used to the new place."

"Uh-huh," I said. "Um, what's for breakfast?"

"Breakfast burritos! Ted picked them up this morning after his run. And it's a good thing, too. We haven't had time to do any grocery shopping."

Ted goes running almost every single morning. I don't really get why, but I can't complain when there's delicious food involved.

"Awesome. That sounds perfect," I said.

"Good," my mom replied. "You'll want to eat quickly, though, so you can get started on unpacking. This room has to be all set up before your friends come, and you've got a lot of work to do."

"I know, I know," I said, stretching my arms up high over my head and then letting them flop back down with a thump. "But there are so many boxes! Are you sure you can't help?"

My mom laughed. "You're kidding, right? You're lucky you only have to unpack one room. Ted and I are dealing with the rest of the house. And believe me—that's no easy task."

"Okay, fine," I grumbled. "I suppose you have a point."

After my mom left I headed for the bathroom and splashed some cold water on my face. Then I dug around in the large cardboard box labeled BATHROOM SUPPLIES until I found a towel and my toothbrush and toothpaste. I also unpacked everything else in the box—my soap, washcloths, and towels—while I was there. One box down and ten to go!

Next I ran downstairs. Our new staircase was curved in the shape of a C, unlike our old one that had gone simply straight up and down. *I like the curviness*, I decided as I headed for the kitchen. But there was something else I liked even more and I couldn't help but smile as I gazed out at it: our new swimming pool. I'd never had my own pool before, and this particular pool was awesome. It was a big rectangle—perfect for swimming laps or just lounging around on a raft—and the water seemed extra blue and sparkly. All I wanted to do was cannonball in immediately!

Seems like Pepper was enjoying the pool too. He's a black-and-white mutt with about twelve tons of energy. He's super-lovable and mostly well behaved, but he has been known to rip a doughnut straight out of my hands, and sometimes he can't help but jump on me when I come home from school. And speaking of Pepper misbehaving, at the moment he was outside lapping up water from the pool.

"Is he allowed to do that?" I asked my mom, pointing at Pepper through the sliding glass door that led outside.

My mom looked up from her coffee, gazed outside, and frowned. "Probably not. I think the chlorine is bad for his stomach. And his fur could get caught in the drain, which can't be good for the filtration system."

She stood, opened the door, and called for Pepper. He came right into the kitchen with his tail wagging, probably because he smelled food.

"Morning, Pepper," I said, giving his neck a good scratch. "How do you like our new digs?"

"Please don't say the word 'dig,'" my mom whispered. "I don't want to give him any ideas."

"What kind of ideas?" I asked.

"Well, the last thing I want is for Pepper to dig up the new garden."

I looked at the green grass outside, still totally confused. "What new garden?"

"The new vegetable garden I'm going to plant as soon as I get the inside of this house settled. You know, after I finish my semester of teaching and make sure everything is set up for the new baby and finish reading Proust like I've been meaning to do for the past ten years."

"Oh," I said. My mom has been talking about reading Proust forever, and I don't even know who she is. I took a bite of my burrito. Some salsa dripped onto my chin, and I grabbed a napkin and wiped it off. "Good luck with that."

Pepper whimpered and placed his head in my lap. His scruffy fur was still damp from the pool, so now my favorite baby blue, super-soft flannel pajamas had a giant wet spot. "Ugh, Pep. You smell like a wet dog!" I said, gently pushing his face away from me.

“That’s because he is a wet dog,” my mom pointed out.

“Um, yeah. Thanks for stating the obvious,” I replied. “The problem is, I smell like a wet dog now too.”

I went to take another bite of my burrito, but Pepper seemed to have the same idea.

“No jumping,” I said firmly as I held my food up over my head. “Pepper, no.”

Even though he backed off, he kept staring at me with his big, brown puppy-dog eyes. It was cute for a second, then sad, and then kind of annoying.

“I don’t know what’s better,” I said. “Having a dog begging for my burrito inside the house, or having him drink chlorinated water on the outside.”

“I’ll take care of him,” said my mom, getting up and grabbing Pepper by the collar. “Let’s go back outside, buddy.” She led him toward the door and put him in the yard.

Once outside Pepper found a red-tailed squirrel to chase.

“Poor animal probably once had a peaceful existence,” I said as Pepper barked up at our gigantic avocado tree. “Then the Weeble-Stevens move to town!”

“Well, at least it’ll have to get some exercise now,” my mom pointed out as she took a small sip of coffee. “That’s one chubby squirrel!”

I chewed the final bite of my burrito, crumpled the

wrapper into a tight ball, and looked around. “Where’s the trash can?” I asked.

My mom glanced around too, bewildered. “I suppose we haven’t unpacked it yet. Why don’t you leave it on the table for now? I’ll figure something out.”

“Okay,” I said with a shrug. “I guess I should get going. I’ve got a lot of work to do.”

I headed back upstairs and actually paused at the top of the steps because I forgot which direction my room was in. When I looked to the right, I saw four doors and when I looked to the left, I saw four doors. In our old house, there was no looking to the left at the top of the steps. All the rooms were to the right. This place was literally twice the size of our old house, and it was going to take some time to get used to.

Once I finally figured out where to go—left and all the way to the end of the hall, I kneeled in front of the first box. It was labeled GIRL’S CLOTHES.

“Yup, I would be the girl in this scenario,” I thought as I peeled off the tape and pulled open the flaps on top. The box was stuffed full of winter clothes. And since it was only April—not even summertime—I shoved the box into the corner of my closet.

The next two boxes of “Girl’s Clothes” were filled with bathing suits, bras, and underwear. I put all my stuff away in the lowest drawer of my dresser. Then I unpacked all my T-shirts and shorts. Dresses came next—I hung them in the closet once I found the hangers at the bottom of the box. And then I unpacked my jeans and pants and leggings. The box after that was labeled MISC., which is short for miscellaneous, which means stuff that doesn't fall into any real category but is decidedly not junk.

I found a few old notes from my friends, a roll of duct tape with purple and red hearts all over it, my science fair project on bugs and their color preferences, a few birthday cards from last year, an old roll of stamps, and a pair of black glasses with a big plastic nose and mustache attached to it.

"How's it going, Annabelle?" my mom asked, poking her head into my room.

I slipped on the glasses. "Who's there?" I asked. "I can't see a thing!"

"Very cute," she said with a laugh. "But I'm glad to see you're making progress. Why don't you use an empty box for the things you don't need anymore?"

"Okay, good idea," I said as I tossed an old red sweatshirt into the closest empty box.

"I thought that was your favorite!" my mom said.

"It used to be, but it has a gigantic hole in the sleeve."

My mom picked up the sweatshirt and inspected the damage. "Oh, that's just along the seam. I can get that fixed if you want."

"Okay, sounds good," I said. "Thanks."

My mom wished me luck and left, and moments later my phone vibrated with a new text.

It was from Oliver Banks, my boyfriend.

Oh, yeah—that was another exciting development in my life. I had a new boyfriend. And having a boyfriend, in general, was brand-new for me. Oliver was my first and he was super-cute and sweet, too. And guess what else? Now that I'd moved, he lived right down the street—only eight houses away.

*How r trix?* he wrote.

*Great!!!* I texted back. Then I frowned down at the screen of my phone, wondering if I'd used too many exclamation marks. Three seemed like an awful lot.

Uh-oh . . .

The more I thought about it, the more uneasy I felt. I didn't want to scare Oliver or appear to be yelling at him or anything.

Yikes. I kind of wished there was a way to take one of the exclamation marks back. Ideally two. Or maybe even one exclamation mark was one too many.

If Oliver mentioned them or acted weird, maybe I could tell him my finger had accidentally pressed the button one too many times. Or two too many times—I wasn't really sure which would be more acceptable.

Or maybe it was okay to be excited because moving was exciting. Right?

Except how excited should I allow myself to be? Too much enthusiasm could be construed as weird and/or not cool. It's not that my life is all about appearing cool—it's so not! But at the same time, I didn't want to act like a big dork, or even a little dork. Any kind of dorkiness is best to be avoided. That's a good motto to live by—especially in middle school.

I stared at my phone. Why wasn't Oliver writing me back?

Why, why, why?

Had I already wrecked things?

Did my boyfriend think I was an overenthusiastic dork? Of course he did. No other explanation made sense.

Gah! I couldn't believe how badly I'd messed up. Oliver and I had been officially together for less than two months. And already it was over.

All because of a text.

And not even a whole text.

This was all about the punctuation.

I flopped down backward on my bed and stared up at the ceiling, wishing I could start the day over.

But no—I'd ruined everything with those three exclamation marks. This was the beginning of the end!

Photo: Jimmy Bruch

**Leslie Margolis** is the author of many books for young readers, including the very popular Annabelle Unleashed series—consisting of *Boys Are Dogs*, *Girls Acting Catty*, *Everybody Bugs Out*, *One Tough Chick*, and *Monkey Business*—and two other Maggie Brooklyn Mysteries: *Girl's Best Friend* and *Vanishing Acts*. *Boys are Dogs* is the inspiration for the Disney Channel original movie *Zapped*, starring Zendaya. She lives with her family in Los Angeles, California.

www.lesliemargolis.com
www.maggiebrooklyn.com